The Happy Life of Preston Katt

ALSO BY J. J. ZERR

The Ensign Locker
Sundown Town Duty Station
Noble Deeds

The Happy Life of Preston Katt

a novel

J. J. Zerr

THE HAPPY LIFE OF PRESTON KATT
A NOVEL

Copyright © 2015 J. J. Zerr.

All rights reserved. No part of this book may be used or reproduced by any means, graphic, electronic, or mechanical, including photocopying, recording, taping or by any information storage retrieval system without the written permission of the publisher except in the case of brief quotations embodied in critical articles and reviews.

This is a work of fiction. Character names are products of the author's imagination. Ship names, as well, are fictionalized, with the exception of aircraft carrier and battleship names, where the actual names of the vessels were used. The story's setting, however, was intended to be historically accurate as to dates, times, and locales of major battles and events.

iUniverse books may be ordered through booksellers or by contacting:

iUniverse
1663 Liberty Drive
Bloomington, IN 47403
www.iuniverse.com
1-800-Authors (1-800-288-4677)

Because of the dynamic nature of the Internet, any web addresses or links contained in this book may have changed since publication and may no longer be valid. The views expressed in this work are solely those of the author and do not necessarily reflect the views of the publisher, and the publisher hereby disclaims any responsibility for them.

Any people depicted in stock imagery provided by Thinkstock are models, and such images are being used for illustrative purposes only. Certain stock imagery © Thinkstock.

ISBN: 978-1-4917-6233-2 (sc)
ISBN: 978-1-4917-6235-6 (hc)
ISBN: 978-1-4917-6234-9 (e)

Library of Congress Control Number: 2015904250

Print information available on the last page.

iUniverse rev. date: 4/29/2015

To Don Graveman and World War II vets of the front and home front

THANKS:

To Karen for a discerning eye and a gazillion other things;
To AHHA Studios STL for cover concept;
To my Coffee and Critique bubbas and bubbettes;
To Margo;
To Lou for Proverbs 12:1;
To Tom Jenks.

If I could have absorbed even half of what all of you labored to teach me, there'd be no faults with this story. Alas. And those are all mine and none yours.

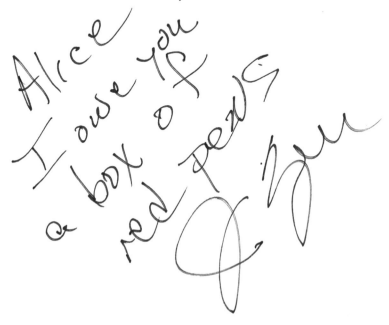

1

DECEMBER 7, 1941

The sky above the black Pacific, the island of Oahu, and the Pearl Harbor naval base was so filled with stars that it appeared to be more an upside-down bowl coated with glowing milk than spotted with distinct pinpoints of light. Occasionally, the overfull heavens dropped a star, and it fell to earth trailing a streak of fire, a death scream the eye could hear.

On the naval base, battleships, all sporting proud lights, ringed Ford Island like a lei of illumination. Across the harbor, cruisers, destroyers, and support ships crowded the piers.

On each naval vessel, sailors stood watch—*at* their posts more than *on* watch at 0200 and only halfway through the endurance exercise of the midnight-to-0400 watch, the midwatch.

Pier D1 was farthest from the ocean and near the fence separating the base from civilian Oahu. At the head of D1, a couple of pole lights illuminated the fronts of buildings as if they were movie-set facades. A single pole light illuminated the harbor end of D1. Darkness cloaked the middle of the pier. The four destroyers tied to D1 slept as soundly and soundlessly as dead, deserted hulks. However, one of the destroyers at the harbor end, USS *Callahan*, though appearing as deserted as the other ships, thrummed with energy and power. The other ships were cold iron, drawing electric and steam life from the pier. *Callahan* was ready destroyer and had to be able to get under way with thirty minutes' notice. On her, huge blowers sucked air in to support the fires in her boilers. The smokestacks whooshed exhaust gases into the night. *Callahan* was awake. Not so the three watch standers manning *Callahan's* quarterdeck. The light of day separated them—a chief petty officer, a second-class petty officer, and a seaman first class—considerably by rank, but the midwatch had numbed their brains equally after the hours on duty in the middle of the night, watching for an enemy who never came and for important officers who sure as hell would never come at that time of morning. The brains of all three ached and buzzed with fatigue and encased a walnut-sized core of wakefulness fueled only by teeth-gritting determination. *Callahan*'s quarterdeck was located on the stern.

Abeam the bow of *Callahan* and under pier D1, invisible in the impenetrable blackness, two sailors sat side by side in a punt. They were awake. Wide awake. Earlier that afternoon, Seaman Seconds Katt and Moriarity had used the punt—a short, stubby rowboat—for its intended purpose, painting the side of a ship along the waterline.

As they'd worked, Katt followed Moriarity's lead, and they'd dragged the task out so they could tie the punt off at the bow of their tin can at "knock-off-ship's work." Then at 2300, an hour after taps, Moriarity led Katt to the dark bow. Moriarity didn't seem worried at all, but Katt's heart hammered so hard he worried someone would hear it and catch them sneaking off the ship. Moriarity told Katt to climb down the rope first, and he managed to do so without falling off the rope and into the water. Then the two had paddled under the pier to shore, snuck along the beach, and crawled through a hole in the fence for a rendezvous with two Japanese girls and a bottle of rum at a swatch of sand two hundred yards from the fence. Palm trees framed the swatch. Picnic tables provided a tropical parlor for the social interaction between the young ladies and the sailors. After a second rum and pineapple juice, which Moriarity had taken from the galley, Katt's worry diminished. The girl Moriarity had given him set about to earn the money she had been promised, and she erased the rest of his worry.

About 0100, the rum and the juice—along with the rubbers, and the money in Katt's pocket—ran out. As the girls departed, the gravity of what he'd done hit Katt with a splash of sudden, cold sobriety.

"You worry too much," Moriarity said. "I'll get you back aboard. No sweat."

As he followed Moriarity back through the fence to the punt, Katt's anxiety increased with every step, with every silent paddle dip to the spot opposite the bow of *Callahan*. As they'd glided quietly past the destroyer in front of theirs, the USS *Spenser* had seemed dead, deserted. One light glowed at the quarterdeck watch station, which was between the after gun mount and the superstructure. Inside the hulls of destroyers, as inside the larger cruisers and the behemoth battleships, much of a warship's vitals resided on and below the main deck, such as guns, boilers, turbines to turn the propellers, fuel and water storage tanks, ammo magazines, berthing spaces for officers, chief petty officers, and enlisted men, administrative offices, sick bay, and the mess decks for enlisted and the wardroom for officers. The only design feature of their ship of concern to Katt and Moriarity, however, was the eighteen-foot distance from the water to the deck on the bow. They had to climb a rope to get there. *And please, God*, Katt thought, *without being caught*. As ready destroyer, the ship was required to have its crew—all of it—aboard.

"Nothin' to worry about, Katt," Moriarity had told him. "You know how it is. People turn into zombies on the midwatch. We won't have any trouble sneaking back aboard. Trust me."

Moriarity's plan worked great all the way until they were ready to climb back aboard their ship. Then they found one of the watch standers on *Spenser* leaning on the lifeline at the stern smoking and looking at the bow of *Callahan*. There was no way they could climb back aboard without the smoker seeing them. Katt's right leg, the one next to his shipmate, started jigging up and down.

"Hey," Moriarity whispered.

Katt grabbed his leg and forced it to be still. Katt leaned and hissed, "Shh."

"You're such a worrywart," Moriarity said. "He can't hear us whisper."

Katt hadn't even noticed the drone of a diesel motor, a boat on the way to Ford Island probably, and the ripples lapping at the pilings and the sides of the ships on both sides of the pier. Still, the background noise didn't seem like enough to cover Moriarity's whisper. If the guy on *Spenser* had a flashlight …

From the shadow figure on the stern of *Spenser*, the

glowing end of a cigarette arced up and then down into the water and snuffed.

"What'd I tell ya? Nothin' to worry about."

Katt was new to the US Navy. A boot. He was worried even if Moriarity wasn't.

They heard a lighter flick open and saw it flare.

"Shit. He's smokin' another one," Katt whispered.

"Shh." Now Moriarity sounded worried.

Katt's leg started jigging again. *Why did I listen to Moriarity?* It was a fine time to start asking such questions. Katt always listened to Moriarity.

He'd gotten in trouble once before because of it. Before he reported to the *Callahan*, Katt never had a friend. The night he checked aboard, Moriarity was one of the watch standers on the quarterdeck. A burly, six-foot chief petty officer sporting a neat, full, black moustache was OOD, officer of the deck. He glanced over the orders Katt handed him and said, "Seaman Second Class Preston Katt, welcome aboard. You'll be in First Division."

First Division was home to forty deck seamen, the sailors who handled the anchors, mooring lines, the boats—basic sailor duties.

"I'll take him to the berthing compartment," a skinny sailor, as was Katt, and short, about five seven, also like Katt, cut in. "I'll get him set up with a bunk."

The OOD spun and snapped, "No, shitbird. You'll take him to berthing and turn him over to Petty Officer Sampson. Then"—the OOD jabbed the little guy on his chest—"you, Moriarity, will get your duty-shirking, malingering ass right back up here. You got seven and a half minutes."

"Uh, Chief," Katt said. "Tell me how to find it. I don't want to get anybody in trouble."

"It's all right. Moriarity will show you the way. You're not getting him in trouble. That's one thing he don't need no help with. He's in your division. Steer clear of him, though. He's led lots of innocents into deep and serious shit."

First Division berthing was forward, the quarterdeck aft, and Moriarity talked the entire length of the ship. He intrigued Katt. In his experience to that point, life was serious business. Surviving-or-not-surviving serious. Moriarity, however, didn't take anything seriously. That was clear just in the walk down the side of the ship. In ensuing days, he was always at the center of any group, always talking, and life to him seemed to be fun. Katt had no experience with that concept either. Moriarity drew Katt to him with a high-tide gravitational pull.

Katt never drank alcohol before the first time on liberty with Moriarity. Then his *friend* kept buying beers, and he kept drinking them. The next morning, Katt woke in a flophouse hotel room, a puddle of beer-and-peanut puke on the floor beside him. And he got back to the ship three hours late for 0730 muster.

"Why'd you leave me?" Katt asked him.

"A man's got to learn how to handle booze. That was lesson one."

Lesson two came at the hands of the commanding officer at nonjudicial punishment, or captain's mast. The captain was tall, broad shouldered, and wore a face meaner than the nuns Katt'd had in grade school.

"Seaman Second Katt," the CO said, "this is your first

offense against the Uniform Code of Military Justice. I could cut you some slack."

Katt felt his Adam's apple bob as he tried to swallow spit, but his dry mouth couldn't manufacture any.

"But I want to impress on you the seriousness of your most important job. You must be at your appointed place of duty ..." The captain leaned over the podium in front of him, which separated the CO in his role of judge, jury, defense and prosecution attorneys, and executioner from Katt the accused. The CO thundered the rest. "On goddamned time, *every* goddamned time! Do you goddamn understand?"

Katt's punishment had been the loss of half a month's pay and restriction to the ship for a full month for being three hours late, for a first offense.

Sitting in the darkness under D1 and willing the guy on the *Spenser* to go away with clenched-teeth intensity, Katt cursed himself as heatedly and profanely as any of his division mates would have for listening to Moriarity.

"Tonight," Moriarity had said, "we're going to celebrate you completing your sentence. You're not restricted to the ship anymore."

"But the *Callahan* is designated ready destroyer. The ship has to be ready to get under way quickly. We can't go ashore."

"You're such a boot," Moriarity had said.

He'd made that word *boot* drip with something that shamed Katt. It meant he was worse than a raw recruit. It contained *sissy* and *momma's boy*. It *made* him want or even need Moriarity's approval.

Moriarity had grinned that grin of his. "We're going," he'd said.

Like a raw recruit, sissy, momma's boy ... *No*, Katt thought, *like a totally stupid raw recruit, sissy, momma's boy, I just followed him!*

If they were caught, Katt knew he'd be in big trouble. Katt had reported aboard and promptly gotten himself to captain's mast. He was restricted to the ship for a month. Then the day after the restriction expired, there he was, about to get nailed again for violating the one thing the captain had hammered home: be at your appointed place of duty. The other time, he'd come back late from authorized liberty. Now, with *Callahan* ready destroyer, the crew, all of it, was required to be aboard.

Katt realized then, sitting under the pier, that they had deserted their place of duty. Desertion packed all kinds of serious meaning, like treason. Desertion in time of war was a firing squad offense. At least they weren't at war. Still, so soon after Katt's first appearance at mast, if they were caught, the CO would throw the book at him. He might even get a dishonorable discharge. The new life he'd wanted to carve for himself out of the navy, gone, *poof*. Because he'd followed Moriarity. Because he'd been stupid. Now the leg jigging kicked into high gear. Moriarity hissed at him.

On the *Spenser*, a voice called, "Billings."

The smoker—Billings, apparently—threw his second cigarette away. It landed in the water near the bow of the *Callahan*. The shadow figure on the *Spenser*'s stern sauntered toward the puddle of light forward of the gun mount to the quarterdeck.

Katt couldn't see a thing under the pier, but he knew Moriarity was grinning. They heard mumbled voices from the quarterdeck of the *Spenser.* Maybe Billings had been sent on an errand.

"Let's go," Moriarity said.

A couple of paddle strokes had them beside their ship. Moriarity climbed up the rope and onto the deck. Katt glanced at the stern of *Spenser.* No one there. He tied off the punt and was about to climb up when he heard Moriarity ask, "You got a light?"

Katt froze. He heard a lighter flick open. They'd been so worried about the guy on the *Spenser,* they'd forgotten about the security patrol on their own ship. Besides a quarterdeck watch, every ship maintained a security patrol to guard against problems both below and above decks. The security patrol was armed. Katt gripped the rope, held his breath, and stared up at the lifeline, expecting the security watch stander to look over and find him.

"Thanks," Moriarity's voice came from the other side of the ship.

"Where is it?" Katt couldn't put a name to the voice.

"Where's what?" Moriarity asked.

"I smell booze. Where's the bottle, or does someone have a still going?"

"Sorry, man," Moriarity said. "It was a bottle. It's gone. I tossed it."

"Shit. Being ready destroyer on Saturday night ... shit, Sunday morning, it's just the shits, you know?"

Katt let go of the rope with one hand to still his spastic leg.

"Gimme a drag." The voice was on the far side of the ship too.

A few seconds later, he heard "Hey!" from Moriarity. "Why'd you throw the smoke away?"

"Why didn't you save me a snort?" the other voice asked.

"Sorry, man."

"Oh, you're sorry, all right, Moriarity. A sorry asshole."

Katt heard a watertight door bang shut.

Moriarity leaned over the lifeline above him and waved a hand to come up. Katt climbed like a hungry monkey with a bead on a banana.

"We made it," Moriarity said. "Let's get below."

"You go," Katt said, and he sat on a bitt, one of a pair of short steel posts with mooring lines coiled around them.

"Suit yourself," Moriarity said and left.

Katt let out a big breath and looked up. He was surprised to find a half moon up there, which seemed to him subdued by all the stars, as if it barely had enough power to define itself against all the light backdropping it. Katt felt exhausted, wrung out, and he dropped his chin onto his chest as he thought over how it might have played out. The security patrol could have looked over the side, seen a dark figure climbing a line, pulled his .45, jacked a shell into the chamber …

He could've been shot. Or maybe they'd just have grabbed him. Katt could see Moriarity shrugging and denying any connection to Katt's criminal activity.

Katt's right leg started up again.

How did I let this happen to me?

He'd enlisted to get away from Saint Ambrose, Missouri, and his momma. She'd been a drunk all the while he was growing up. And although she'd been sober, mostly, during his senior year of high school and managed to hold down a job for the entire year, he was terrified he'd turn out like her if he didn't get away. But then he checked into the *Callahan* and tangled up with Moriarity. He'd allowed Moriarity to twice lead him into—

"O my God," he whispered. "I am heartily sorry for having offended Thee."

He determined to turn his life around, then and there, not wait for years and years as Momma had.

Lifting his eyes back to the moon, he thought he understood how Lazarus felt when they unwrapped the sheet from his face and he could see the world again.

"Jesus, Mary, and Joseph," he prayed to the half of a heavenly body. "I will not have anything to do with Moriarity. Ever again. I will not sit with him on the mess decks. I will not go on liberty with him. I sure as shit, God, will *never* do anything like this with him again!"

"Um, and I'll work on the cussin'."

He felt a little better. A better way forward was in front of him. Then he thought about the girl he'd been with. He saw her future, and it turned into a vision of his momma and the men he'd found her with so many times when he came home from school.

Katt rested his elbows on his knees and thought about the sins he'd have to confess. The things he'd done with the girl—he'd been with a whore. It was ugly to stick that word on a woman, but what he'd done stuck more than ugliness on his soul. It stuck eternal damnation there.

He leaned forward and placed his face in his hands.

The security patrol found him like that and shook his shoulder.

Katt looked up.

"What're you doing?" the sailor asked Katt.

"Just sitting here. Is there something wrong with that?"

"You're the dumb-ass new guy. Yeah, there's something wrong with you sitting here. I want to be in bed, but I can't. You can be in bed, but you ain't. That pisses me off. Get the hell below."

Katt did as he was told. When he got into his bunk, he lay there awhile as his troubles continued to boil in his head. He didn't think he'd be able to sleep. If he didn't sleep, the next day would be a long one.

DECEMBER 7, 1941

From pier D1 at 0540, USS *Callahan* appeared to be asleep. Inside the hull and below the main deck, however, engineers were moving around boilers and pumps checking gauge readings, and in the galley amidships on the main deck, cooks were almost finished preparing breakfast. In the First Division berthing space, the eyes of the senior enlisted man in the division, First Class Petty Officer Sampson, popped open. He didn't need a watch or clock to tell him the time. He lay on his bunk and listened to the sounds of his sailors. There were a couple of snorers, there was a whimperer, and there were always a few turning over and rustling the sheets. And a moaner reliving the ecstasy of rented love ashore. Sampson smiled. His sailors called him a hard-ass. What would they say if they knew he woke early every morning to wallow for a moment or two in affection for *his* sailors? Of course, he also woke early to get in and out of the head before the pack of teenaged bodies jammed the small space for their shit, shower, and shave.

Sampson's bunk was the center in a tier of three near the rear of the compartment. He swung out, and his feet splatted on the tile. He was wearing only white skivvy drawers, and his upper body was hard muscled from the time he spent lifting weights. His legs, however, were spindly and didn't appear to be up to the task of supporting the thick chest. Sampson grabbed his toiletries kit from his locker, dropped his skivvies, and tied a towel around his waist. As he did every morning, he took a moment to check the berthing space before going forward for his three *S*s.

The space was crammed with bunks in tiers of three and stacks of three-foot-high aluminum lockers, these in tiers of two. There were three narrow aisles between the bunks and lockers. Dim red lights, which didn't ruin night vision, gave off just enough illumination to distinguish the main features of the space's layout. With everything in order, he went to claim sole possession of the head for seven minutes. He was at his bunk and dressed in clean skivvies at 0600.

The ship's announcing system blared, "Reveille, reveille. All hands heave out and trice up. The smoking lamp is lit in all authorized spaces."

Katt, in his top bunk, put his arm across his eyes, shielding them from the stabbing overhead white lights. He groaned.

Around him, a chorus of voices damned reveille, the ship's announcing system, and Molasses. Molasses was a slow-walking, slow-talking petty officer from First Division who had the watch that morning and was therefore responsible for inviting sailors to "rise and shine."

Katt's head ached. The taste of pineapple and tin stuck to his tongue, and he felt queasy and hoped he wouldn't throw up. Every commode, urinal, and sink would be occupied in the bathroom—which the damned navy insisted be called a head.

Katt winced at "Drop your cocks and grab your socks."

Goddamned First Class Boatswain Mate Sampson bellowed the same thing every weekday morning in port and on weekends when the destroyer *Callahan* was required to be able to get under way at short notice, like that morning.

"I'm going to get a cup of coffee," Sampson said. "When I come back, if I find one of you pimple pickers still in the rack, I will kick your ass up around your ears."

A couple of bunk tiers from Katt, Moriarity said, "Those toothpick legs of yours ain't gonna kick nobody's ass." After a pause, he added, "Petty Officer Sampson."

Even hungover, even finding the sense of repentance he'd gone to sleep with was still with him, Katt admired Moriarity and his ability to mouth off but to stay just to the safe side of trouble.

Katt put his hands over his ears when Sampson hollered, "Well, then, Seaman Second Moriarity, how about I rip your arm off and beat you with the bloody stump?"

"How about that, Moriarity?" one of the guys asked.

That sounded too damned cheerful, Katt thought. He waited for the guys in the two bunks below him to crawl out. Then he joined the mass of grumbling, groaning, growling bodies clad only in white skivvy drawers, carrying Dopp kits and towels and jamming the narrow aisles between tiers of bunks.

"You look like shit," Moriarity said from behind him.

"Serves me right for going with you."

"Listen, after the head, hustle up to the mess decks and eat some fried potatoes."

"I don't want to eat anything. I'll puke."

"Eat the potatoes. Trust me."

Katt ate fried potatoes not because he trusted Moriarity.

He thought maybe the potatoes really would make him puke. Maybe that would get the poison out of his belly. The potatoes were greasy. Puking seemed imminent for a moment. But he ate a couple of hard, black, charred slices, and they settled his stomach. He ate more. It didn't happen instantly, but halfway through his large serving, Katt was surprised to discover his headache was gone. Gone too from his mouth was the pineapple-and-tin taste that had overpowered his toothpaste a minute after he finished brushing. He wasn't going to puke. And he was hungry.

By the time muster rolled around at 0730, Katt was feeling good, as only a person who has had recent experience with total-body misery can feel good. After the muster was completed, Sampson gave Katt and Moriarity their work assignment.

"I want you back in the punt at 0805."

At precisely 0800, a whistle would blow, and everything would stop. On every ship around the harbor, and at every flagpole ashore, the Stars and Stripes would be raised. After the flag was hoisted, three whistle blasts sounded—"Carry on." After that, on the ships and around the naval base, work began.

"You two took all day working the starboard side yesterday," Sampson continued. "You *will* finish the port side by noon today. Otherwise, when we get rid of the ready destroyer duty at 0805 tomorrow, you two numb-nuts will not get your liberty cards."

Even if he got his liberty card the next morning, Katt had no intention of using it. He had no desire to revisit the terrors and miseries he'd experienced after his last foray ashore.

Moriarity grabbed Katt's skinny bicep. "Come on. Let's get down to the paint locker before the line forms. I want my liberty card tomorrow."

"The hell with a liberty card," Katt said, pulling his arm free. "I don't have any money left. Payday is a week from tomorrow."

"We can borrow money," Moriarity said.

"Sure. Borrow ten bucks, and on payday, pay back fourteen. That's stupid."

"It's not stupid. We'll probably go out to sea for a couple of weeks. It's easy to pay it back out there."

"I am not borrowing money."

"Well, you better not screw up *my* liberty," Moriarity tried to growl, "or I'll kick your ass up around your ears."

Katt laughed. Moriarity was five eight, an inch taller than he was, and the same weight. Katt weighed 125 in his skivvies.

Moriarity stomped away. Katt hurried after him. The other guys would beat the crap out of him if he tried to cut ahead in the line at the paint locker to catch up to his shipmate.

Under the bow, the chain locker housed the anchor chains, and aft of that sat the paint locker, not much more than a coat closet crammed with buckets of paint, brushes, and chipping hammers. The third-class boatswain mate in charge was Molasses. After being relieved as quarterdeck watch, he had reported to his normal workstation. Watching Molasses make entries in the paint-locker logbook as sailors checked out paint and tools, Katt wondered if Molasses deliberately dragged out his tasks, as if the nickname gave him an excuse to work excruciatingly slowly.

Katt watched the petty officer's lips move as he spelled out chipping hammer. *C.* Then slowly, deliberately, he inscribed the letter in the book. *H.*

Two men were in line for the paint locker ahead of Katt and Moriarity when the ship's announcing system blared, "Now hear this. The ship will get under way in thirty minutes. All hands man sea-detail stations. Now hear this," and the message was repeated.

Katt had never been to sea with his ship.

"So we're on port lookout, right?" Katt asked. "And you'll show me what to do?"

"Course I'll show you, but it's starboard lookout," Moriarity said with a grin that worried Katt. The grin indicated Moriarity thought going to sea detail was a lark, not serious at all. "First," Moriarity went on, "we gotta change into whites. Getting under way, we can't be in dungarees."

Up two ladders, back onto the forecastle and across to starboard, and then aft and down a ladder. The berthing space was again jammed with bodies, all roiling like a nest of snakes. It took a bit of shoving and a lot of cursing for Katt to make it to his locker and fight the door open and pull out a uniform. Going back to his bunk, he waded through a gauntlet of jabbing, stabbing elbows. He climbed up onto his bunk and got dressed there.

Moriarity, in his whites, was waiting on the port side of the main deck underneath the whaleboat suspended in a davit above him.

A sudden loud roar of airplane engines made Katt wince. He looked up but couldn't see anything from under the whaleboat. A *whoomp* sound was followed a second later by pressure on his ears.

Then the general quarters alarm sounded.

Katt didn't know what to do. Moriarity grabbed his arm and pulled him toward the set of ladders leading up one deck. At the 01—the "oh one," one deck above main deck—Moriarity cut across the ship to another ladder and up to the 02 level and the starboard lookout station just outboard of the pilothouse. Moriarity's job was to stand the post. Katt's was to observe, to learn how to be a lookout.

They arrived at the tiny space, and Katt glanced up. Buzzing planes swarmed across the blue sky.

"Zeros," Moriarity said. "Couple of those are zeros!"

Pretty high up, Katt thought. Some planes flew level. Some dove on Ford Island behind the *Callahan*. Explosion after explosion blew. Sharp *crack*s, baritone *baboom*s, and others more pressure and vibration than noise. Black smoke billowed from the stern of the nearest battleship. Katt had no idea which one it was. Two geysers erupted near the smoking battlewagon, near misses.

"Japs," Moriarity said. "Get your goddamned Mae West on. And your helmet. You stay here. I'm going to shoot some a those slant-eyed sons of bitches."

"Wait," Katt said. "I don't know what to do."

Moriarity grinned. "Figure it out," he said and headed down and aft.

Against a cacophony of airplane engine droning and the explosions, a single machine gun *tattatatt*ed. Katt thought it sounded lonesome and lost. Then a twin five-inch gun mount boomed from the side of the smoking battleship. A cloud of water erupted from the bow of the same ship. A low-flying plane sporting a red circle on the side of the tail buzzed into view from the left and disappeared behind the *Callahan*'s smokestacks. *A Jap, all right.*

"Starboard lookout, report."

The voice had come from a brass tube fixed to the bulwark, a chest-high wall of steel in front of him.

"Starboard lookout, report."

Through the window of the pilothouse, Katt saw Sampson glaring at him. He leaned down to the voice tube. "Here, sir."

"You're supposed to say, 'Manned and ready,' dipshit," Sampson said into the voice tube in front of him.

"Manned and ready … sir."

Katt felt as if most of his brain was frozen, as if rational thought was an immense distance beyond where he could reach, but he'd caught himself, just in time.

Through the voice tube, Katt heard the bridge team stepping through preparations for getting under way.

The door to the pilothouse ripped open, and Sampson charged out.

"Where's Moriarity?"

"He went to shoot a Jap, sir."

"That shitbird." Sampson opened an aluminum bin mounted to the bulwark and pulled out a set of sound-powered phones and plugged the cord into a receptacle. "You do know what this is, right?"

"A sound-powered phone, sir. Doesn't need electricity," Katt said as he dredged up a lecture he'd sat through in boot camp. "Navy ships might receive battle damage and lose electric power, and we still have to be able to talk over our phones. So—"

"Jesus Christ, Katt," Sampson bellowed. "It's a sound-powered phone. That's all you had to say."

"Yes, sir," Katt said. "And this is the PL circuit—phone lookout, sir."

"Newbies! Damned Moriarity. Okay, Katt." Sampson took a breath and let it out, "My fault. What I should have asked was, do you know how to use the PL?"

"Yes, sir." He pulled the earphones over his head and slung the strap around his neck. The strap connected to a small metal plate with a microphone attached to it. "And when I want to talk, I push this button on the microphone."

"Okay, Katt. But you just cover one ear with the earphones. You have to have the other open to hear the voice tube. And"—Sampson's forefinger jabbed Katt's chest above his life vest—"this is important. You see something, make your first report through the voice tube. The officer of the deck needs to hear your report first. Then you make the report over the PL circuit. Got it?"

"Yes, sir."

"You call an officer *sir*. Me, call me *bosun*, not *sir*. And if that shithead friend of yours isn't back by the time we get under way, I'm going to—"

A series of explosions, the largest yet, from the direction of Ford Island were followed by wafts of concussive pressure.

There were three battleships in view, and they bloomed with yellow-orange fire that fed clouds of rising black smoke. The nearest one was down at the bow and listing.

"Katt," Sampson said, "keep your head outta your ass. Do the best you can."

As Sampson hustled back into the pilothouse, Katt

looked aft at Ford Island, and for a second, he wondered if he were dreaming. Explosions, fire, guns booming, machine guns, planes dropping bombs, dumping torpedoes. And so close but at the same time far enough away that it could be a dream or a movie.

Over the sound-powered phone, Katt heard, "You know what the hell's going on?"

Voice 2: "The Japs are blowing the shit out of things. That's what the hell's going on."

Voice 1: "No. I mean we were going to get under way before the shit hit the fan."

Voice 3: "The word is a Jap sub was spotted inside the harbor. Inside!"

Up on the bow, someone swung a fire ax, chopping through the mooring lines. Normally, sailors from other ships or the naval station pulled the lines in from the pier. Today, the pier lay abandoned. On the other destroyers along D1, a lot of sailors scurried, as if motion and speed were their only objectives.

Katt heard a Thompson chatter from the fantail. The *Callahan*'s gun in the after five-inch mount fired, and the recoil sledgehammered through the hull. Then suddenly, it was quiet. Guns had stopped firing. Glancing up at the sky empty of planes, he wondered, *Is it over?*

The ship started backing away from the pier. A deck above him, he saw the captain lean over the rail, looking aft.

"All engines stop," the CO ordered.

Katt felt the vibration of the propellers thrumming through the hull cease. Funny, he hadn't noticed the thrum until it ceased. The feeling that something was funny didn't last long. As he stared aft, it seemed idiotic to get closer to all that destruction behind them, but that's what they were doing. The stern of the *Callahan* was drawing closer to the burning battleship across the harbor from pier D1. As they coasted toward it, a huge explosion ripped apart the middle of the battleship. Chunks of steel flew up into the air, twisting and tumbling ahead of a billowing cloud of steam and more black smoke.

Katt cringed, inclined to duck behind the bulwark, but he couldn't tear his eyes from where pieces of the battleship raining from the sky frothed the water a ship length away.

Another swarm of planes buzzed into view and dove on targets on the far side of Ford Island. All around him, things were happening. He asked himself, *As a lookout, shouldn't I report what I'm seeing?* But it seemed stupid to say anything. There was too much to look at. Besides, the planes, the explosions, the fires, they were so obvious.

Katt jerked his head left and then right. His feet turned him in a complete circle. The sky was filled with airplanes. The planes were bombing the shit out of ships around Ford Island. Not one of the planes was hit.

The captain called for engines ahead two-thirds, and Katt felt the vibration of propellers biting water. The bow of the *Callahan* began to swing to line up with the outbound channel. *The Japs'll see us moving*, flashed through Katt's mind. But the planes were all diving on the battleships. That realization steadied his nerves some.

Sampson poked his head out the door of the pilothouse and hollered at him. "There's a Jap sub inside the harbor. Understand? Inside the harbor. Find it." A disgusted expression came over the boatswain's face, and he charged onto the lookout station, pulled binoculars out of the aluminum bin, and thrust them into Katt's hand. "Find the goddamned sub."

Katt pulled the eyepiece covers off, glanced around for a place to put them, and finally dropped them in the storage bin.

Through the binocs, the world was blurry. *Shit. Focus knob.* He rolled the knob one way and then the other. The world crystallized sharp and—

A straight silver line on the surface of the blue harbor was pointing right at the *Callahan*. He'd never seen one before, but there was no question about what it was.

"Torpedo! Dead ahead!" Katt bellowed into the brass tube.

The torpedo had them nailed. It was going to strike the bow. Over the voice tube, he heard, "Hard left rudder. Engines ahead flank."

The bow started swinging left, away from pointing directly at the torpedo. Then the bow stopped. Now the torpedo was coming right for where Katt stood. It would strike exactly beneath him.

Katt closed his eyes. *O my God, I am heartily sorry. I've been whoring. I've been drinking. I cussed. I didn't send money to Momma.*

It felt like his eyes had been closed a long time. He opened them. The ship was turning right now. The captain must have turned the ship to make the torpedo miss, he thought.

Peering down, a narrow silver wake traversed along the side of the ship, missing them by a few feet. The torpedo continued drawing its trail on the water until it slammed into the shore and exploded.

They blew up that picnic table where the Japanese girls—

A picture of Sampson flashed into his head, saying, "Keep your head outta your ass."

Katt spun around and got the binocs up. There, following the wake, he saw something, a stick above the water.

"Starboard lookout has a periscope, five degrees off the port bow!" he hollered into the voice tube.

Katt saw part of the sub's conning tower above water. He saw the *Callahan*'s forward gun mount trundle over to the bearing of the sub. The barrel lowered and stopped. But it didn't shoot.

"Shoot the goddamned gun!" Katt hollered.

"It's too close in." Sampson was behind him. "The gunners can't depress it that low."

The bow crept left.

"We're gonna ram it," Katt said matter-of-factly.

Sampson said, "If he has another torp—"

It was a small sub, not even a third of the length of the *Callahan*, Katt thought. The *Callahan* just missed nailing him head-on. The minisub scraped down the destroyer's starboard side with a metal-on-metal grinding, thumping, screeching, a scream almost. When it bobbed past the stern, the *Callahan*'s wake turned the sub sideways.

Sampson said, "Missed the son of a—"

A plume of water twice as wide as the *Callahan*, white at the edges, black in the middle, burst the surface of the harbor behind them with a *whoomp*. The plume shot as high as the mast. The *Callahan*'s stern rose, and Sampson fell against Katt, but they both grabbed on to the bulwark and maintained their footing.

A chunk of metal rode high in the plume. *A piece of the sub?* Katt wondered.

A heavy vibration juddered through the *Callahan*. Over the voice tube, Katt heard the captain order the engines to stop. The vibration diminished gradually as they slowed.

The sky had again emptied itself of planes but not of black smoke. All of Ford Island appeared to be on fire. The depth-charge plume cascaded back into a huge black circle on the surface of the harbor.

The string of battleships lined up nose to tail around Ford Island had been beaten up badly. One was on its side. One had sunk, with just the top of its masts above water. The others had fires burning and listed one direction or the other.

Katt sank to the deck and leaned back against the bulwark. He felt as if he'd been running from something, like he did in a dream sometimes. In the dreams, as long as he ran hard, there was nothing to fear or reason to wake. But he'd stopped, and it caught him. A huge wave of what he'd run from in his dreams washed over him. His right foot started jiggling.

Sampson sat next to him. "Jesus, the battleships! Every one hit. *Arizona* sank. A lot of dead sailors on those battlewagons."

"Are we alive, you think?" Katt asked.

"What?"

"Do you think we're alive?"

"I don't know," Sampson said. "When I can stand up again, I'll ask the captain."

"What do you think he'll say?" Katt asked.

The way Sampson stared at him, Katt might have had two heads. Then the big man slapped a knee. "Newbie!" he exclaimed and laughed hysterically.

"What in hell is so funny?"

Katt and Sampson looked up at their pissed-off commanding officer glaring down at them from the door into the pilothouse. Sampson jumped to his feet. He grabbed Katt's arm and pulled him up.

"Nothing's funny, sir. We, uh … I guess we were just happy to be alive, sir," Sampson said.

The cold hardness washed out of the CO's blue eyes. He nodded, and then he looked back at Ford Island.

Katt looked too. Orange-red fires blazed and fed billowing, dark smoke columns. The battleships. Katt had never been to a circus, but he'd seen a picture of a parade of elephants, their trunks gripping the tail of the beast in front, filing into a circus tent with rows and rows of happy people seated on bleachers. His mind altered the circus image, and he saw the elephants after they'd wobbled out in step, not to a tent full of smiling kids but into a slaughterhouse. The battleships, they were supposed to be all-powerful. Heavily armored. Invincible. Not like thin-skinned destroyers, which were called tin cans. Now all the battleships were dead or dying. The image of gray, slaughtered elephants stuck in Katt's head, overwriting what his eyes took in.

The CO muttered, "Sons of bitches caught us with our pants down this morning. Not gonna happen again." He spun around. "Sampson, get back to your post. Lookout, find me another goddamned Jap sub."

Sampson started following the CO into the pilothouse, stopped, and turned to Katt. "Find a Jap sub, the CO said."

Katt faced forward. The *Callahan* was coasting toward the entrance to Pearl Harbor. Palm trees backdropped strips of white sand to both sides of the channel with the blue

Pacific beyond. He brought the glasses up and studied the surface carefully. No stick periscopes.

Boots stomped up the ladder behind him. A grinning Moriarity asked him, "How'd you do?"

"You left me here," Katt said. "I didn't know what to do."

Katt's indignation didn't touch Moriarity's exuberance. "Word is," he said, "the executive officer was on the fantail. The XO watched the sub scrape down the side, and then he ordered setting two depth charges to go off at thirty feet and to drop them. Chief Petty Officer Swanson was in charge of the depth-charge crew, and he argued, 'We'll blow ourselves up.' The XO tripped the releases, anyway." Moriarity grinned, just as he had earlier. "Word is, we were lucky as hell those depth charges didn't blow in the ass end of our ship. But we got the sub, and all the *Callahan* lost was one blade off the starboard propeller."

"This is the captain," they heard over the ship's announcing system. "We killed that damned Jap sub. And Seaman Moriarity shot down a torpedo plane with a Thompson. I've put him in for a medal, and I'm promoting him to seaman first."

There was a pause, as if the CO was thinking of what to say next. Katt stared at Moriarity. In a crisis, Moriarity had known what to do and did it. Katt had to be kicked in the ass by Boatswain Sampson. Moriarity shrugged as if it were no big deal.

The CO continued, "We did lose a blade off the starboard propeller. The engineers are locking that shaft as we speak. As soon as they're done, we get under way on the port propeller. Our job will be to patrol the approaches to

Pearl Harbor, see if there are more of these sons of bitches trying to sneak into our harbor.

"One more thing. The job you all did today, it was so damned close to satisfactory work. I am just proud as shit to be your shipmate."

The crew roared, and Katt heard it twice, once with his uncovered ear, once over circuit PL.

Moriarity shook his head. "Cap'n's sumpin', isn't he? Other guys would say, 'Damned fine job, men.'"

"Captain says satisfactory is as good as a man can do," Katt contributed, adding, "Sh … um, a promotion and a medal. That's … satisfactory."

Moriarity grinned. "Listen to this. That goddamned gunner's mate in charge of the ship's armory wanted to place me on report for burning up the barrels of two machine guns and expending the ship's entire annual peacetime allowance of .45 caliber ammo.

"The captain told him yesterday was the last day of peace. 'Order us some goddamned war bullets, gunner.'"

After three days of sub patrols along the south coast of Oahu, the *Callahan* returned to pier D1. Shipyard workers set about replacing the starboard propeller. Seaman Second Katt and Seaman First Moriarity manned the punt and repainted the entire waterline. The Jap sub had ruined the paint job on the starboard side they completed the day before they got under way.

"Dad-burned Japs," Katt said.

3
DECEMBER 21, 1941

The cloudless royal-blue sky over the deep-blue Pacific, the air so clear one could see the horizon as the edge of a flat earth, two weeks into the war—such a day squeezed sailors with anxiety. Enemy eyes at periscopes, enemy eyes behind aircrew goggles, enemy eyes peering through binoculars could see forever in such conditions.

But even clouds and reduced visibility wouldn't have been able to hide Task Force Eleven. Fifteen US Navy warships were arrayed across a box of ocean two miles to a side. Light winds prevailed and were unable to sully the deep blue with white-capped waves. The task force, however, steamed fast as it zigzagged around a westerly course; and each ship dropped a wide white runner across the cobalt sea; and each wake congealed with others to paint a wide, white arrow, which would magnetically pull enemy eyes to the task force's position.

The aircraft carrier USS *Saratoga* was the center of the force. Three heavy cruisers maintained stations a thousand yards to the front and sides of her. Three thousand yards in front of the carrier, six destroyers formed an arc-shaped screen. Forming the rear were an oiler and four additional destroyers, including the *Callahan*.

On the mess decks of the *Callahan*, Katt sat with Seamen Firsts Peterson and Wyatt. The high speed of the propellers thrummed through the deck, through the soles of Katt's shoes.

"Three goddamned days we been hauling ass outta Hawaii. Still don't know where the hell we're going," Peterson growled.

Katt often thought hulking Peterson resembled a bear. Short black hair. Perpetual scowl. Sloped shoulders.

They'd finished eating. Most of the crew had. They didn't have to hurry.

Katt said, "Thought you didn't care where we were going as long as Japs were there so we could get back at 'em for Pearl."

"Yeah, but it's been three goddamned days," Peterson repeated.

"I'm worried about what will happen if we find them," Katt said. "The word is the Japs have a lot more carriers than we do."

"Doesn't make a shit," Peterson said. "We're not sleeping on a Sunday morning now. We're at war." Peterson drained his coffee cup. "Still I wish I knew where the hell we're going."

Wyatt shrugged. "When they want us to know, they'll tell us."

A little smile tweaked the corners of Katt's lips. Leave it to Wyatt to sound a voice of reason. A slender six-footer who wore black-rimmed glasses and always had a book in his hands.

A tray plunked onto the table. Katt looked up as Moriarity flopped onto the vacant seat. "We're going to Wake," he said.

"Where's that?" Wyatt asked.

Katt was surprised. He thought Wyatt knew just about everything.

"What is it?" Peterson asked.

Katt rolled his eyes. Moriarity was hard to shut up normally, much less when others encouraged him.

Moriarity said the Japanese attacked Wake Island the same day they attacked Pearl, though on Wake, the fighting occurred on December 8, as Wake resided on the other side of the international date line from Pearl. Daily Japanese bombing raids continued until December 11. Then the Japanese attempted a landing, which the US Marine defenders repulsed.

"Japs are coming back. So we're on our way to bail out the jarheads," Moriarity said.

"We been steaming hard for three days," Wyatt said. "How far is the place?"

Katt knew Moriarity didn't know the answer. He waited to see what kind of baloney his buddy would spin.

"Couple of more days. Course, the admiral could slow down or turn. Who the hell knows what an admiral will do?"

The next day at 1600, the task force did turn—all the way to an easterly heading to return to Pearl Harbor.

"The Japs sent several carriers to Wake," Moriarity told his shipmates. "We only got *Sara*."

"Yeah, but drive all the way out here. Then we just turn chicken and go back home and wait for the sons of bitches to hit us again!" Peterson fumed. "Damned admirals."

Katt thought Peterson had a point. Katt glanced at Wyatt to see if he would chime in, but he didn't.

On the return track, the *Callahan* was one of six destroyers in screen positions ahead of the USS *Saratoga*.

The morning after the task force reversed course, Katt was at his starboard lookout station. The sun had not yet peeked above the horizon, but a smear of red on low, ragged clouds above the only slice of visible horizon announced where it would shortly. Katt rested his binoculars on the bulwark and leaned to peer through them, but there was a vibration through the hull that prevented a stable image.

"Dad-burned XO," Katt muttered.

"What have you got against the XO?" he heard from behind him.

Uh-oh! The captain!

Katt spun around and snapped to attention. The captain was more than six feet tall and thick chested. He was always frowning, sort of like Peterson.

The captain asked him again.

"Um, well, sir, since the Jap attack on Pearl, when the XO dropped the two depth charges, there's this vibration through the hull. Moriarity said he used to be able to rest the binocs on the bulwark and see a long ways. Now with this vibe, well … I can just hold them, but it's not as good as resting them here."

The captain rubbed his chin. "You noticed that vibration, did you?"

"My shipmate did, sir. Makes a big difference in bad light, he says. I think he's right."

The captain reached for the binoculars, and Katt gave them over.

Resting his hand palm up on the bulwark, the CO laid

the binocs across his palm and scrunched his neck down to peer through the eyepieces.

"Try it that way," he said, handing them back.

Katt tried it the captain's way but couldn't twist his arm around the way the CO had. Katt was too short. He laid his palm on the bulwark, laid the binocs across his knuckles, and peered through. He adjusted the focus knob away from the captain's setting. The blurry world crystallized into sharp clarity. And he saw it.

"Periscope," Katt said without taking his eyes away from the binocs. "It's a goddamned periscope!"

"Give me those."

Katt handed the binocs over. The captain peered through and adjusted the focus. "Where?" he asked.

"Dead ahead, sir."

"I don't see a damn thing."

Katt took the glass back, settled it as he had before, and peered.

"Periscope. Clear as shit, sir."

"You're sure?"

"It's a goddamn periscope, Cap'n."

"Sound general quarters!" the captain hollered into the pilothouse. "Officer of the deck, come left ten degrees. Junior officer of the deck, signal the task force: periscope bearing zero niner zero."

The captain grabbed Katt's shoulder. "Watch him. When you think he has drifted five more degrees off the bow, let me know."

Katt stared so intently, it felt as if the binoculars were sucking the eyeballs out of his face. He glanced up to better judge the angle off the bow and then back through the glasses.

He could hear the captain talking to the combat information center about the periscope. He wanted them to calculate the range of the sub. Katt didn't know how CIC could do that. Moriarity had told him about CIC once. "They do magic shit in there, man."

"That's about five degrees, Cap'n. Uh, you know I'm pulling that outta my ass, right, sir?"

The captain was busy on the phone with CIC for a moment, and then he hung up.

"Still there? Uh, Katt, right?"

Without taking his eyes from the binocs, he said, "Still there, Cap'n."

"Let me see."

Katt stepped aside but kept his hand on the bulwark supporting the glasses. The captain peered through them, adjusted the focus, peered some more.

"Son of a bitch."

The captain stood up straight. "Officer of the deck, come right fifteen degrees."

Turning back to his lookout, he stared a moment, shook his head, smiled, and handed the binocs to Katt.

"Nice job," the captain said. "You got some kind of eyeballs. But he might not be the only one."

When the captain smiled, a jolt of pride coursed through Katt's veins. After *nice job*, he got back to his job, scanning the entire half circle on his side of the ship, working deliberately, carefully. The last thing he wanted to do was disappoint his CO. Katt found no other enemy.

The *Callahan* and another destroyer were ordered to attack the sub as the task force steamed away, heading northeast for a distance and then resuming the zigzag around the easterly base heading. For four hours, the two ships ran sub-hunting patterns over the spot where the periscope disappeared. They churned the surface of the Pacific with a number of depth charges, depleting over half their inventories. Just as the two destroyers were about to rejoin the task force, an oil slick was spotted near the eddy swirling above the *Callahan's* last depth charge explosion.

The two destroyers renewed their attacks. No other signs of sub damage were noted, though, and with depth bomb inventories depleted by 80 percent, the *Callahan* led the other ship on an easterly heading back to Pearl Harbor. After the high-speed attacks, both destroyers were low on fuel. They steamed at an economical speed of fifteen knots. The task force was estimated to be 150 miles ahead of them and still going three knots faster.

When the *Callahan* was under way and not at battle stations, Katt stood watch from 0400 to 0800 and from 1600 to 2000. The evening after the ship had attacked the sub, he climbed into his bunk at 2200 and immediately fell asleep.

From deepest sleep, he was ripped awake with a feeling he'd fallen off the earth and was dropping into a deep hole with red glowing from the pit. *Hell,* he thought, and he thought about His just punishments. He'd vowed to quit cussing. That morning, he'd cussed again. He got caught up in the periscope. And he cussed. *Nobody to blame but my own darned self.*

His inch-thick mattress arrested his descent. The mumbles and curses rumbling around him—along with clatters, clangs, bangs, and thumps—returned Katt to his dim red-lit berthing space.

"Weather's gone to shit, boys," Sampson said. "But it's just a little bitty storm. Moriarity, Katt, you two numb-nuts check out the berthing space for loose equipment. Secure anything hard. Doesn't have to be big to hurt somebody. Flashlights, lock for a locker. Secure anything hard. Copy, Moriarity?"

Moriarity mumbled something that sounded negative, but he started moving.

"Molasses, you grab a guy and check the paint locker. Wyatt and Peterson, come with me. We gotta make sure things are secure in the passageway."

Twenty minutes later, everyone was back in the berthing space. "You top-bunk guys," Sampson said. "Stick your arms between your mattress and your bunk. Squeeze your mattress to you like you did the hula dancers in Pearl."

Katt did as told, and it helped some. Still, he couldn't sleep more than a few seconds before the unnatural sensation of falling jerked him up and out of slumber. He was relieved when a messenger informed him it was time to wake up for his four to eight. As he climbed down from his bunk, the ship rolled, and he fell onto his butt. Most of the ship's motion had been pitching up and down. Now it rolled too, and at times, the stern yawed. A kid in the middle of a tier of bunks aft of him leaned over the side and puked onto the deck. Katt grabbed his clothes and shoes and struggled to stand and fought to move toward the head to get dressed there. He had to hold on to something all the time. Arriving, he found the deck awash with seawater. Geysers erupted from the commodes each time the bow rose and fell. A guy was sitting on a commode, and he flushed it continuously to avoid getting befouled by his own poop.

Katt sat on the deck and dressed in the passageway outside the head. Then he started up, fighting g-forces and rolls. In the passageways, he banged bulkhead to bulkhead. On the ladders, he staggered up when the forces pushing and pulling on him let up for brief seconds to gain a step or two on the ladder. Finally, he made his way to the pilothouse.

Sampson handed him a life preserver and a rain poncho. "Be careful when you go out to relieve the lookout. When you get out on the platform, the guy out there will untie his safety line. Don't waste any time getting it tied to you."

Katt pushed against the pilothouse door, but it wouldn't open. He leaned his weight and pushed, and the door opened to winds that roared and ripped at his rain gear. The wind slammed the door behind him. He thought for a moment the gale would pick him up, blow him clean past the stern, and drop him into the raging seas.

Why the hell do we need a lookout?

To the side, he peered into pitch blackness. Facing ahead, the wind-driven rain and spray stung his face like bees from a comb-robbed hive. He couldn't open his eyes. The destroyer with them, the *Spenser*, was in trail. He couldn't see anything back there either. It was stupid. Manning the station in these conditions served no purpose. The damned navy had lookout stations. Lookout stations had to be manned. Didn't the US Navy know there was this word *but*? *But* sometimes things are so bad you don't have to man the outside posts. The officers were supposed to be smart. College boys. They were smart, all right. Sailors stood duty outside. They didn't.

Normally, the boatswain relieved the lookouts every thirty minutes. Binoculars wore your eyeballs out after prolonged staring through them. He hadn't taken the binocs out of the bin, but he thought he had to have been out there longer than thirty minutes. He cursed the boatswain for not sending someone else to take the watch for a while, the weather for beating the shit and freezing the shit out of him, and the navy for not being a land-based service. Then he noticed that as he stepped around his tiny post, when he got close to the window separating him from the pilothouse, the ferocity of the wind and rain diminished. In the shelter of the ship's structure, he could actually see forward.

Well, isn't this swell? he asked himself. He could see all the way to the bow. Holding his hand up to his forehead, it shielded his eyes somewhat from the pelting droplets. It was still dark as hell, but at least he could see a little. He set about doing his job, scanning, without the useless binocs, from behind to abeam and working aft again, forcing himself to go slowly, to be careful with every degree he scanned. Then he worked abeam to dead ahead, and he was about to start swinging his gaze back again.

A shadow. Something solid against a huge wave, rising like a wall of water dead ahead. Wall of water. A picture of Moses leading Israelites through the Red Sea blinked on in his head. Then it blinked out.

A destroyer. Close. Jesus, Mary—

They were going to hit it! There was a cover over the voice tube. Katt ripped it off.

"Ship dead ahead! We're gonna hit the son of a bitch!" he yelled into the tube.

Katt's eyes locked onto what had to be the *Spenser*. Katt

had the sensation the *Spenser* and the *Callahan* were on separate teeter-totters. The stern of the *Spenser* dropped in sync with the bow of the *Callahan* sinking. Then the stern of *Spenser* would rise abruptly, and the screws would pop out of the water as she slid into a trough, and the bow of *Callahan* would rise, and Katt would lose sight of the other ship for a moment.

How did the *Spenser* get in front of the *Callahan*?

Katt didn't know. What he did know was that the *Spenser* inched closer and closer as she teeter-tottered on the huge waves just in front. In these seas, would anyone survive a collision?

Then Katt saw the bow of the *Callahan* begin to edge to the right relative to the other ship. At first he thought it wasn't enough. The two vessels would still crash together. But they cleared.

Father, Son, Holy Ghost! I mean, thank you, man, or men, or whatever, or whoever the hell all you guys are!

The stern of the other destroyer danced down the port side of the *Callahan*. The last view he had was of the *Spenser*'s screws out of the water and spinning as if they were mad as hell they couldn't chew up the *Callahan*.

The *Callahan* rolled violently and far to the right. Katt leaned against the bulwark. He thought he could touch the surface of the ocean if he just reached his hand out. From somewhere, his mind dredged up the fact that the bridge was forty-two feet above the surface. From his post, he could touch the surface of the ocean.

Time stopped.

Katt stared at the water. It was going to swallow him. He'd be dead. Was that okay or not? *I should be afraid* passed through his mind. He was above the ocean, leaning on the bulwark with all his weight. And the ocean was right there. An impulse to dip a hand in the water rose in him, but he was afraid. Everything was so delicately balanced in the middle of the raging storm.

Katt saw only seawater. It was without color. Color wasn't important. Space, time, place, everything was frozen as if he were looking at a picture.

The ship shuddered. Slowly it began to right itself. The rollback accelerated and sped through upright to thirty degrees of heel to port. Abruptly, the roll reversed again, and Katt smacked back into the side of the ship. Inside his head, a lightning crack flashed and extinguished, and utter blackness filled him with a void.

Katt felt his eyelids flutter. Had a second passed or half an eternity? It didn't matter. Time, a thing that didn't matter.

White glowed everywhere. It was everything. He wasn't sure if his eyes were open or closed.

"Katt?"

The voice was stern, authoritative. Almighty.

"Here I am, Lord."

4

JANUARY 2, 1942

Eight bells sounded over the *Callahan*'s announcing system: noontime. In sick bay, Moriarity straddled a metal folding chair. His arms rested on the back.

Sick bay was about the size of the paint locker, but where the paint locker was on the second deck, ill lit, and jammed with buckets and cans of paint—many half full and gilded with dried dribbles and runs, along with other buckets filled with brushes and chipping hammers stuffed onto the stacks of paint—sick bay gave the impression of a bright, open space. Located on the main deck forward of the mess decks, starboard side, the space had a porthole, the cover of which was open, and two overhead lights. The tile gleamed. The aluminum gleamed. Aluminum cabinets above aluminum counters above aluminum drawers, all gleamed. Still, sick bay was a narrow space with barely room for two sailors to pass side by side between the polished metal fixtures mounted to the fore and aft bulkheads. In sick bay, First Class Hospital Corpsman Duffy had set broken bones, dealt with cuts requiring stitches, treated venereal disease and cases of infestation from head lice to crabs, and treated walking pneumonia and severe athlete's foot. Duffy's general quarters station was in the wardroom, where he could use the officers' dinner table as an operating platform.

From his chair, Moriarity, dressed in whites with his Dixie-cup hat on the back of his head, peered up at Duffy. Duffy wore dungarees, leaned against an aluminum counter, and had his arms crossed over his chest.

"Come on, Doc," Moriarity said. "If you go up to the hospital and talk to those guys, they'll listen to you. It's Friday, you know? Nobody does anything over the weekend. I tried to talk to them, but those hospital guys won't listen to a seaman."

"Go to your division officer," Duffy said. "Get him to go up to the hospital."

"I talked to Petty Officer Sampson, Doc," Moriarity said. "Sampson said the quacks at the hospital won't listen to a boatswain mate, and they sure as hell won't listen to a boar-tit ensign. 'Gotta be another quack,' Sampson said."

"I'm not a doctor," Duffy replied. "I barely qualify as a nurse."

"Bullshit, Doc. Everybody knows you are what you need to be. Everybody knows you even took a kid's appendix out once. The quacks up at the hospital will listen to you."

"They won't listen to me. Jesus, don't you know what they've been through since December 7? Burn cases, bullet wounds, amputations, some kids off their rockers after what happened to them, and not near enough doctors and nurses to deal with it all."

"Doc, you know Katt's okay. You saw him yesterday, and you said he was okay."

"Yeah, Moriarity, he appeared to be okay to me, but

Katt had a concussion. He needs a real doctor to say he's okay. And right now, they're too busy to get to Katt."

Moriarity looked down at the deck for a moment, and then he stood up and glared at Doc Duffy.

"Since the Japs attacked, everybody's busy. Everybody's working their asses off."

Duffy dropped his arms and stood up straight too.

"If you don't do something, Doc, we're never going to see Katt again. The *Callahan* pulls out on Monday. When they finally get off their asses up at the hospital and some quack finally checks him and says, 'Oh, yeah. This one's okay. Release him,' we'll be gone, and they'll send him to another ship. Shit. Maybe they'll send him to an oiler. Katt's meant to be on a warship, on a tin can."

"I'm in dungarees," Doc Duffy said.

That was the lamest excuse Moriarity had ever heard. It wouldn't take any effort at all to change into whites. He glared hard into Duffy's eyes. Duffy fidgeted. He was the oldest guy on the ship, damned near fifty, Moriarity recalled. Duffy was a really nice guy with a sort of puffy body. Looking at him, you'd never picture him cutting out someone's appendix on the wardroom table.

Moriarity was ready to threaten getting a couple of guys from First Division to stuff Duffy into his whites and carry him to the hospital. But Duffy had caved. Moriarity could see it his eyes.

"Shit," Duffy said.

Moriarity grinned. "Me and a couple of guys will meet you on the quarterdeck, Doc. We'll bring a uniform for Katt."

Katt was sure he was okay. He didn't need to go to the hospital in the first place, but Duffy had insisted a real doctor see him. Getting in the hospital was easy. Getting out, that was tough.

"Sorry, Seaman Second," they said to him. "All the doctors are busy right now." Day after day after day they said that.

Then he saw Moriarity and Duffy striding down the aisle between the beds of the long, narrow ward. Shortly after they arrived, a doctor came. He shined a light in Katt's eyes, asked some questions, and okayed Katt's release from the hospital.

The doctor left, and Moriarity handed the uniform he'd brought to Katt.

"Hustle it up," Moriarity said. "Get dressed."

Katt pulled his pants on. Then he said, "I don't know what they did with the uniform I wore when I came here."

"The hell with it," Moriarity said. "Let's get out of here before that doctor changes his mind."

"But—"

"But, my ass," Moriarity said. "Hustle it up."

Katt stood up after tying his shoes and saw Duffy walking away.

"Hey, Doc," Katt said. "Thanks. Thanks for getting me out of here."

Doc stopped, turned around, and nodded to Katt. Then Doc turned and glared at Moriarity for a moment before spinning on his heel and stomping away between the ranks of beds. There were twenty against each wall—bulkhead, actually, Katt corrected himself. In the US Navy, even in an ashore hospital, structures were comprised of decks, bulkheads, and overheads.

Katt pulled his jumper on. "I think Doc was expecting you to say thanks," he said to Moriarity.

"For doing his damned job?"

Katt and Moriarity met Wyatt and Peterson in the hospital reception area, and the four spilled out the door. On the sidewalk outside the main entrance, Peterson punched Katt lightly on the shoulder. Wyatt grinned at him.

"Knock off the grab-assing," Moriarity said. "We got to get someplace. I hear Primos calling us."

"Moriarity, wait," Katt said. "All I want to do is to go back to the ship."

"Bullshit. You're not going to the ship," Moriarity said. "We gotta celebrate busting you outta of this place."

"Yeah," Peterson said. "We were afraid we wouldn't ever see you again. We gotta celebrate. Hell. You never know. We mighta missed ya."

"You want to go back, Katt," Wyatt said. "I'll go with you."

"Ain't nobody going back," Moriarity said. "There's this neat bar I heard about. Just the place to celebrate the return of our little lost sheep to the fold."

Katt protested some more, but his protestation wasn't up to task of dissuading Moriarity.

Moriarity grabbed Katt's arm and pulled him across Makalapa Boulevard to a bus stop opposite the one that took riders to the naval base and Honolulu. As they waited for the bus, Moriarity and Peterson babbled about something

Molasses had done. Katt was thinking about his resolutions, how many times he'd made one to not go on liberty with Moriarity, and here he was again.

A bus came. No one got off. Katt followed Moriarity onto a full bus. Two brown-skinned men occupied every bench seat. The look on the brown faces, from bus front to rear, told Katt he and his buddies did not belong there. Of course, Moriarity didn't seem concerned.

The bus lurched into motion, and the four standing sailors swayed as they hung on to overhead bars. White houses, some with picket fences, all with a palm tree and flowering bushes snuggled against them, floated past the window for a couple of minutes.

Then the last of the houses slid behind, and Katt saw grassy rising terrain to his right and the same long-stem grass waving in the breeze falling away to the left with the ocean visible, perhaps a mile away. The driver was brown skinned too, Katt noticed. The buzz of conversation started up behind where Katt stood hanging on to the overhead bar near the front of the bus. After about ten minutes, peering around Peterson in front of him, Katt saw a dense collection of small houses on the right side of the road and some distance ahead.

Katt heard Moriarity ask, "You guys work at the navy base?"

"Navy base," a voice affirmed.

"You guys do great work," Moriarity said. "If you're going to the Paniola Bar, I'll buy you a beer."

The conversational buzz dried up, just like when they'd boarded the bus, Katt thought. The bus slowed and turned off the road, boiling up a cloud of red dust in its wake.

The brakes screeched, and then the bus stopped. The door accordioned open.

"This is it," Moriarity said. "Get off, Wyatt."

Once on the ground, Katt moved toward the rear of the bus where Wyatt and Peterson waited. A steady stream of men filed out of the bus and began trudging up a red dirt road arrowed up the sloping hillside. The road bisected an orderly formation of houses.

Moriarity stepped down from the bus. One of the Hawaiians was talking to him.

"Listen, Haole, you don't want to go in that Paniola Bar." Katt followed the man's pointing finger. "Halfway up the hill is another bar, much nicer place. It's called Lupe's. A Japanese used to own it, but they took him away. Lupe took it over. Lupe's. Much nicer place."

The man got into the stream of men flowing uphill. The bus pulled away. Katt waved his hand at the stirred-up dust.

Across the road from the bus stop and down a short dirt road running between stunted palm trees sat a single, faded, white, wooden rectangular shed with a low-pitched tin roof. A faded sign tacked to the center of the roof read Paniola Bar. There was a door under the sign and two large windows to either side. The windows appeared to have been painted black. A number of motorcycles and a couple of battered pickup trucks filled the dirt lot in front of the place.

Katt grabbed Moriarity's arm. "Let's go to Lupe's, like that guy said."

Moriarity grinned, lifted Katt's hand off, and crossed the road with Peterson beside him. Wyatt looked at Katt and shrugged. Katt and Wyatt checked both ways, and then they followed their leader.

After winding through the pack of parked motorcycles, Moriarity pushed open the door and entered. A loud hubbub of voices quit abruptly. Katt followed Peterson inside and found four tables with six to eight large, brown-skinned men on chairs at each, all staring at him, at them. They'd boarded the bus to "You don't belong here" looks. These guys were giving off "You don't belong here" with menace.

Pitchers of beer and glasses filled each occupied table. There was a short bar with four stools. Two of those were occupied. Cigarette smoke fogged the air. There was a pool table against a far wall. No one was using it.

A table right in front of them was unoccupied. It had six chairs. Moriarity pulled one out and sat.

Wyatt sat next to him, and asked, "'Paniola'—do you know what that means?"

"Hawaiian for cowboy," Moriarity said. "But see that? It's all bamboo and fake flowers up there around the bar. Hawaiian cowboys ain't from Texas, that I can tell ya."

Peterson brought a pitcher of ice water from the bar and plunked it in the center of the table.

"Katt," Moriarity said, "since you're on first-name basis with the Almighty, have him change this water into beer."

Katt blushed as the others roared.

Peterson said, "Here I am, Lord."

After the fresh laughter died down, Wyatt said, "The Doc says, 'Katt.'"

"Here I am, Lord!" the three shouted.

Before the new round of laughter died, Wyatt sauntered to the bar and returned with two pitchers of Primo.

A hulking guy in shorts and a T-shirt strolled up to the table, right behind Wyatt.

"You guys gonna continue to make so much noise?" the big man asked.

"Oh, no, sir," Moriarity said. "We're just celebrating our buddy here." He hooked his thumb at Katt. "He just got out of the hospital. We'll be real quiet now we told him how happy we are to see him again."

Katt could see the man weighing Moriarity's wiseass response, weighing whether it was enough to go ahead and beat the hell out of him and anyone else who cared to pitch in. The man's gaze flicked to Katt. Those hard, black eyes conveyed hostility of a kind he'd seen before. When he was growing up, he came home from school at times to find a man with Momma. The men had eyes just like this Hawaiian cowboy. Katt had learned to quickly look away from those eyes. And he did there in the Paniola Bar. After a moment, Mr. Hostility walked away.

Katt saw Moriarity following the man with his eyes, and before his shipmate could wise off again, Katt said, "Let it go, please?"

Wyatt poured Katt a glass of beer.

"My doc said no booze."

"Lying sack of shit," Moriarity said. "Drink the damn beer. We're here celebrating you getting out of the hospital."

"Let him alone, Moriarity," Wyatt said, and to Katt, "I'll get you a Coke."

Halfway through the second pitcher of beer—most of both had been consumed by Moriarity and Peterson—the big guy came back with two of his like-sized buddies.

So Katt wouldn't wind up injured again, Wyatt hustled

him out of the Paniola Bar. Moriarity wound up in the naval hospital with a broken jaw. Peterson was hauled away by the shore patrol. Two weeks later, after the *Callahan* returned from a round-trip to the West Coast, Katt visited his shipmate and brought the notification that the captain had busted Moriarity back to seaman second.

His starboard lookout station—that's how Katt'd come to think of it. It occurred to him that he was happy there when his ship was at sea. The realization surprised him. When he thought back over his years in grade school and high school, he could see that his only focus had been on survival. There had been nothing to be happy about—or sad either. The only things in his mind were how to find food to eat and clothes to wear. In high school, he added studying so that he could get away from Saint Ambrose, Missouri, his mother, and becoming just like her. Now, he found happiness on that tiny platform outside the pilothouse on the *Callahan*.

There was guilt too. He knew he wouldn't be there if it hadn't been for Moriarity pushing Doc Duffy to get him released from the hospital.

Wyatt had told him, "There's nothing for you to feel guilty about. You know how Moriarity is. The rest of us breathe air. He breathes trouble."

The *Callahan* had spent most of early 1942 at sea. She had escorted convoys to the West Coast of the United States, other convoys to Adak in the Aleutians, and still other convoys from there back to Pearl.

After every return to Pearl, Katt visited Moriarity. Moriarity had had to deal with an infection and other difficulties with his jaw healing properly. Duffy told Katt that it would be a matter of luck if they were able to get him back aboard the *Callahan*. So many ships were entering the fleet that there weren't enough sailors to man them.

"The only way we get Moriarity back," Duffy'd said, "is that we have to be there when he's released."

Katt was determined to do for his buddy what Moriarity had done for him.

But now, in early May, the *Callahan* had been assigned to a task group with two aircraft carriers and a lot of cruisers, destroyers, and support ships. The task group had steamed west at high speed.

The ship was at general quarters. Something big was going on, but what it was, Katt didn't have a clue. "We're mushrooms," Moriarity used to say. "They keep us in the dark and feed us shit." But Moriarity was still in the hospital back in Pearl. Nobody else could figure out what was going on the way he did.

Sometimes, *the word* ran around the ship with "This is what's happening." *The word* occasionally turned out to be factually based, but since they'd left Pearl two weeks prior, the task force had steamed west. Beyond that, the word didn't have any more insight into what was going on than the seaman second mushrooms. Moriarity would have figured it out—some of it, anyway.

Anyway, to Katt, it really didn't matter. Steaming across the ocean, manning his post, searching for masts sticking up above the horizon, searching for planes, searching for periscopes—like the one he'd found in December. "Good job." Earning another of those from the CO would be nice.

But there was something extra special going on,

something big. Even a seaman second could figure that out. The navy had committed two carriers, a potload of cruisers, and a massive potload of destroyers to whatever the hell it was they were doing. *It must be the whole darned Pacific Fleet,* Katt thought. Of course, there were no battleships. None of those had been repaired yet.

There were so many good-guy ships around that there didn't seem to be ocean enough for a Jap ship on the scene. "Periscopes and planes, Katt," Sampson said. "Officer of the deck says watch for those."

Straight up, the sky was blue. Horizontally, haze limited visibility. The air appeared to be loaded with watered-down milk mist, and puffy gray-white clouds covered half the sky. Great cover for planes to attack the task force.

If you're up there, Seaman Second Katt will find your Jap ... butts.

His no-more-cussing resolution turned out to be the absolute hardest thing he'd ever tried to do. He had to pay constant attention to his mouth and the words it said. The mouth was easy, though, compared to his thoughts. They seemed more predisposed to cuss than even Moriarity.

Moriarity. He wondered what kind of grief he was giving the nurses and hospital corpsmen back at Pearl.

He went back to searching the sky. In conditions like those they had that day, the naked eye worked best. He picked up the out-of-place black dots or something moving. Then he'd swing the binocs up, and he'd see a bird. He always checked, made sure. Katt didn't cry wolf, except when the dad-burned wolf was really there.

The ship started another turn. They'd been in front of the carrier. The task force made a lot of turns, or rather, the carriers made a lot of turns. They had to face into the wind to launch and recover their airplanes. The whole formation wheeled with the carriers.

At task force center, each carrier had cruisers abeam both sides. The big ships, the carriers and cruisers, rode majestically above the white-capped waves. The *Callahan* and the other destroyers too, Katt saw, rolled like crazy when they wound up in the troughs of the waves. Katt hung on to the bulwark as his ship gyrated through a series of jerky rolls, snapping from one direction to the other. It just made a person angry, that a simple thing like a ship turning around could be so violent that it rendered a person helpless against the power of the sea. And the sun was shining. The seas were not that high. Not at all like that storm the *Callahan* had encountered in December the previous year. It didn't take much of a sea state to toss tiny destroyers around while sailors inside rattled like BBs in a shaken tin can.

The rolls damped out as the formation steadied on course with the *Callahan* directly astern the carrier. Suddenly, the guns on the cruisers and the carriers cut loose. Five inches, smaller stuff with tracer rounds. The line of destroyers forward of the carriers began firing.

He saw a few of the Jap planes the guns fired at. It didn't seem like enough targets to warrant all the firing. The sky filled with red tracers and gray puffs of antiaircraft shell bursts. Jap planes trailed smoke and fire and fell spinning. And splashing. Katt pictured pilots sitting in cockpits filled with flames licking at their Jap faces and screaming until the merciful sea saved them.

Head outta your ass, Katt.

His job was not to watch the show. His job was to find other threats. Raising the binocs—he needed those to find a periscope—he began a sweep. He covered the half circle he was responsible for and had just started a second sweep over the same arc when he caught a glimpse of something a little too dark to be low cloud or haze. He looked away from the binocs for a second and then put them up to his eyes again. A plane. Low flyer.

Katt bent over the voice tube and shouted, "Low-flying aircraft bearing zero nine zero! Twin engine! Coming right for us!"

In the binocs, the plane grew bigger. He couldn't see it through the haze without the glasses.

Why is this goddamned Jap coming for us? he wondered. *We're little, a no-account destroyer.* He wanted to point to the carriers. *There. They're the ones you want.*

The *Callahan*'s gun mounts slewed around to 090. The forward mount fired. The concussion hit Katt like a punch in the chest.

The ship turned hard to the right. Katt bumped against the window to the pilothouse. The two forward gun mounts, fifty-one and fifty-two, pumped out rounds. *Wham, wham.* Katt imagined the inside of the mounts, the gun recoiling, the guys loading the shells and powder charges, the breech mechanism sliding forward. And one mount firing *wham*, and the second mount echoing *wham*. Katt pictured mount fifty-one guys and mount fifty-two guys, the members of both teams pushing each other to not let the dipshits in the other mount pump out more rounds. *Wham, wham.*

Katt brought his eyes back to the bomber. It was boring

in on *him*, like their aiming dot was centered on the poor, simple seaman second on starboard lookout.

The ship heeled more as it accelerated in the turn. The guns spoke. *Wham, wham.* And Katt stared at the plane closing. He saw the bomb bay doors open. He saw the bombs drop—one, two. He saw the two bombs flying for him, the bull's-eye.

Pieces flew off the bomber. The bomber bore on, straight for him. A wing separated, rose, and spun away up and then fell behind the fuselage. The plane started spinning and descending. Katt let go of the binocs. They hung on the strap around his neck. The bombs flew straight and true. The one-winged plane spun with fury at its death, intent on not dying alone. Katt extended his arms as if he were crucified to wood that earthbound mortals could not see.

5

MAY 1942

The fighting had gone on for four days. During each of the four days, the sky above the task force had been filled with an upward-flying rain of antiaircraft fire. Sometimes at night, hundreds of guns flashed and grumbled like summer heat lightning. From the sky, burning Jap planes and Jap bombs fell. Some of the Jap bombs found targets. The task force lost the carrier *Lexington*. The other carrier, the *Yorktown*, absorbed damage, and she was returning to Pearl at high speed with half the task force. The other half steamed at fifteen knots, slowed by battle-damaged vessels. The engagement was being called the Battle of the Coral Sea.

As far as Katt was concerned, he'd been standing through the entire ordeal. When the ship had not been at general quarters, he'd been on watch. Now, though, the task force was headed back to Pearl Harbor. It was 0805, and he was sitting at a table on the mess decks wondering if he was too tired to lift a forkful of scrambled eggs to his mouth.

Wyatt sat down across from him. Two more guys took the other two seats. Katt didn't know their names. They were snipes, though. Snipes worked in the hot, sweaty engineering spaces. They made electricity and water to drink. They made the ship go. He wouldn't want their jobs, especially in the middle of a battle like the one they'd just left. Stuck deep inside the ship, they couldn't see what was happening.

Katt had heard First Division sailors talk about the snipes. "They send me to work down there in a snipe hole, I'm committing suicide," was one sentiment expressed.

Wyatt said, "My feet hurt clean up to my ass." He sipped his coffee. "No, correction—they hurt clean up to my shoulders."

"Feels good to sit down, all right," Katt said.

The snipes didn't say anything.

"Eighteen goddamned hours at GQ yesterday," Wyatt moaned. "I don't even remember how many hours we spent there the day before and the day before that."

"You guys outside? You see what was going on?" one of the snipes asked.

He was pale skinned and red pimpled. Katt felt a touch of sympathy for the guy.

"Yeah," Wyatt said. "Katt's starboard lookout at GQ. I'm port."

"Word I heard," Red Pimples said, "is that we came within a gnat's whisker of buying it."

"No, man, it was half a gnat's whisker," Wyatt said. "Tell 'em, Katt."

"You tell them," Katt said.

Wyatt took a bite of fried potatoes, chewed once or twice, and swallowed.

"The carriers caught most of the attention from the Jap flyers," Wyatt said. "But one bomber came awfully close to sneaking in on us at low altitude and nailing us.

Eagle-Eye Katt here spotted him. Just in time too. Our gunners shot the bomber down, but after it had released the bombs. Like I said, I was on the port side of the pilothouse. Those things sailed right over my head. I heard them whistle past. Scared the shit out of me, man. The ship was in a hard right turn. No sooner had the bombs sailed over my head, when I look up and see this one-winged bomber spinning around and heading right for us. That time, I thought sure we were goners, but the plane crashed into sea, I don't know, maybe fifty yards in front of us. Then the bow sliced the plane in half. That about it, Katt?"

Katt nodded.

"I heard the Japs sunk one of our carriers," Red Pimples said. "Does that mean we lost the battle?"

"Japs lost a carrier too," Wyatt said. "We shot down a potload of their planes. Did we lose the battle? Have to ask an admiral about that."

Wyatt asked Red Pimples about working around the boilers and turbines. Red Pimples asked about other things Wyatt had seen during the battle. Katt tuned them out. He ate slowly and thought about burning planes and burning pilots in the cockpits. So many American sailors died at Pearl Harbor. A thousand just on the *Arizona*. For the last three days, he'd seen Japanese pilots die. In one sense, a handful of flaming wrecks plunging into the Coral Sea weren't enough to make up for Pearl Harbor. But too it didn't seem right to talk about it the way Wyatt and Red Pimples were. Katt didn't want to talk about it. He didn't know how.

The *Callahan* followed a line of destroyers into Pearl Harbor. From his lookout station, Katt saw welders' eyeball-burning spots of fire dotting the ships at the piers and the dry dock opposite Ford Island. He'd heard one of the officers say, "Japs screwed up. If they'd knocked the repair yard out too—"

The *Callahan* came abeam Ford Island. The four battleships moored there appeared as if all was at peace with the world and had been since the end of "the war to end all wars"; but if a person looked, there was the top of the *Arizona*. To some, it might appear to be navy scrap that no longer had use but was too much trouble to pull out and dispose of properly.

To Katt, the ship, the tomb, was also a promise. The Japs killed them, and he'd lived. That day, a few days after the Japs attacked Pearl, the *Callahan* had entered port, and he'd seen the masts of the *Arizona*, and he'd promised sailors on her he'd do their fighting for them. He experienced a moment of regret for not going with Moriarity on December 7 and grabbing a Thompson too. Vividly, he recalled images of the attack, but he couldn't remember if he'd been scared or angry or what. But seeing the *Arizona* mast tops, something as big and hard as Boatswain Sampson's fist sucker-punched up and out of his gut and stuck in his throat. It was a good thing he didn't have to make a lookout report. The lump dissolved, and Katt took a breath.

The ship maneuvered into an end spot on pier D1 at 1600. Mooring lines were secured. A crane dropped the brow into place, and First Division sailors lashed the end of it to the quarterdeck. Liberty call was announced.

Katt was already in whites, and he streamed off with the

early crowd of "liberty hounds," intending to visit Moriarity in the hospital. The hounds were after something else. As they moved down the pier, they bunched themselves closely together, as if they were in formation, except their formation wasn't orderly. Their huddled voices bubbled with giddiness as they talked about beer and babes and beer. Katt trailed behind them. In one sense, he was glad Moriarity was in the naval hospital. If he were there, he'd be with the pack. He'd be leading it and dragging Katt along too.

Moriarity. Katt liked the guy, but he also confused him. One day, he single-handedly attacked Jap planes bombing Pearl, and he was a hero. Then he attacked a two-hundred-pound Hawaiian cowboy, and he was busted back to seaman second. He sprung his buddy Katt out of the hospital, and a half hour later, he almost got Katt another appearance at captain's mast. Wyatt pulled him out of there just in time.

I let Moriarity lead me into trouble. I need Wyatt to pull me out.

At the head of D1, the liberty hounds congregated around the bus stop for Honolulu. Katt marched on past two piers for the hospital bus.

At liberty call that day, there was nothing more important than visiting Moriarity, but as much as he wanted to see his friend, he worried too. What if Moriarity was okay to go on liberty? Wyatt wouldn't be with them to keep them—or at least Katt—out of trouble.

A bus pulled up, and Katt boarded. Only two other guys were on it. Katt sat near the front and stared out the window. He wasn't seeing Oahu though. He was picturing Saint Ambrose, Missouri, and growing up. He remembered Sister Ralph, his third-, fourth-, and fifth-grade teacher.

Before he entered her classroom, his only memories were of hunger, teeth-chattering cold, and fear. Sister Ralph got other students' mothers to donate clothes for him. She brought a baloney sandwich and a cookie from the convent for his lunches. He studied hard—not to take his report card home; Momma never checked a report card of his—he studied to see the smile on Sister Ralph's face when she handed him his marks. Then, in fifth grade, he began delivering papers for Mrs. Grossman. She ran the grocery store and the post office and managed the delivery of the two Saint Louis newspapers. At first, Momma took all the money he made. When Mrs. Grossman found out, she started a savings account for Preston. When Preston had no money to give Momma, she beat him. Mrs. Grossman told Momma she'd call the sheriff if she beat Preston again.

Katt could not imagine what his life would have been if he hadn't met Sister Ralph and Mrs. Grossman.

The bus stopped by the hospital. Katt stepped off, crossed Makalapa Boulevard, and entered the reception area. A second-class hospital corpsman sat on a stool behind a high counter. Katt asked him if Seaman Moriarity was still in ward C, where he'd been before.

The petty officer pulled a binder from below and opened it on the counter. He ran his finger down the *M* pages.

"Not here," the petty officer said.

He flipped to the back of the folder and again ran his finger from top to bottom.

"Here he is. Seaman Second Moriarity was discharged. A week ago. He had orders to the *Yorktown*."

"I didn't see any carriers in port," Katt said. "So he's out at sea?"

"I don't know about that. Only what's in here," the petty officer said as he patted the binder.

Back outside, back on the bus, back to looking out the window.

He wished he could have pushed things as Moriarity had so that his friend could have stayed with the *Callahan.*

A sense of relief infiltrated his head. Moriarity was gone. He would no longer compel Katt to accompany him on his escapades. Sins, he recalled, could be deeds, words, or thoughts. Guilt formed, and his feeling of relief sank as if in quicksand.

He thought about Seaman Second Moriarity among the sea of bodies on the huge ship. Would he get lost and be unable to find his bunk or the mess decks? Where would he work?

I bet he finds a way to work on the flight deck with the planes.

Moriarity—the guy made Katt smile, mostly.

Back on the naval base, Katt stepped off the bus, and it roared away. Across the street from the stop, Katt spotted a small, white wooden cross over the door of a Quonset hut. When he'd gone to the hospital, he hadn't noticed the cross. Now he saw that on the opposite end of the roof of the hut, a small, white painted plywood box impersonated a steeple.

Katt crossed the street and found the door open. It was a chapel, all right. He considered going in, but his stomach growled. It was chow time on the *Callahan.*

The next morning at 0515, Katt entered the Quonset hut chapel and took a seat on a folding metal chair at the rear.

Along the sides of the hut, the Seabees, he figured, had cut out space to put in pointed-arch stained-glass windows. The windows were glass but not much stained. Up by the altar, a sacristy lamp, a candle inside a red-glass cylinder, glowed. There wasn't much light in the rear, but two overhead spotlights shone on the altar. Looking around, the place did not in the least resemble his church at home with its statues, high and low altars, stations of the cross, stonework, ornate painting scheme, and real stained glass. There had been so much artwork that he hadn't really taken it all in—or even a part of it. It rested in his head as a jumble, a fancy one, but a jumble all the same. The Quonset hut, though, was elegant in its simplicity. In the early Hawaiian morning, before reveille roused the crews of ships tied to the piers, it felt like a church. It felt like a place God might like to spend the night in.

He thought about the *Arizona*, about her masts sticking above the water and all the sailors entombed below. He thought about the skies above the Coral Sea filled with flak and planes falling and trailing smoke and fire and Jap pilots' faces framed in flesh-eating flames. He thought about Moriarity on a flattop. At Pearl, the Japs targeted the battleships. Now, he knew, they specifically targeted the aircraft carriers.

A muted reveille call sounded from a ship.

"Thanks for the visit, Sir," Katt said and left.

As he approached D1, he heard a ship announce, "Under way. Shift colors." The *Callahan* was the only ship at the pier. He started running and held up his ID card for the guard at the lift bar. The seaman laughed as he waved Katt through.

A rough hand grabbed Katt's arm and jerked him to a stop. Katt almost said something, but he saw it was a tall lieutenant commander holding his arm. The man was a lean six-footer. A seabag stood on the pier beside him.

"*Callahan?*" the officer asked.

"Yes, sir. Who are you?"

"I'm the CO."

"Like hell you're the CO."

Katt jerked free and ran as hard as he could.

"Get your ass back here, sailor!"

The *Callahan* was backing and had cleared about half its length. Katt ran harder. The bow was just clearing the end of D1 when Katt ran off the pier, hit the water, and went under. He clawed his way to the surface and started stroking toward the ship, which had stopped backing and had begun to swing to the outbound channel.

Katt heard his name being called, and he stopped stroking and looked up. Boatswain Sampson was on the bow with a heaving line. Sampson pitched it, and Katt wound it around his hand. The deck crew towed him to the side of the ship, dropped a heavier line to him, and hauled him aboard.

"What happened, Bosun?" Katt asked. "We weren't ready destroyer. Why'd we get under way?"

Sampson put his hands on hips. "You, Seaman Second Katt, made a mess on my forecastle. Get a mop." Then Sampson grinned and walked away, shaking his head and muttering and laughing. He stopped once and looked back at Katt, and Katt figured he looked pretty funny with his plastered hair and his whites clinging to his beanpole frame and the puddle at his feet.

Wyatt was next to Katt, coiling the heaving line.

"What the hell would we do for a laugh around here without you, Katt?" Wyatt asked.

Katt asked Wyatt, "Why'd we pull out?"

"Hell if I know," Wyatt said. "Something's going on. Somebody probably realized we weren't involved and he said, 'Holy shit! We'll lose the war without the mighty *Callahan*.'"

Katt plugged in his phone and checked in for his 0400 lookout watch.

"Two days hauling ass. Wonder where we're going?" It was Wyatt, the port lookout. "You guys in combat know? You're supposed to know everything."

"One thing we found out was yesterday there was this big-ass carrier battle. Word is we sank four of theirs." It sounded like the kid named Arlen in CIC. "*Yorktown* got hit, though—"

The rest of the words dribbled off into a drone. Katt went numb. He thought about walking away. Only there was no place to go. *Please, God. Moriarity—*

Over the phone circuit, a rough voice growled, "This is Chief Burns from combat. You shitbirds knock off the chatter, and you goddamned lookouts look out. I'm coming out there. You'd best be doing the business."

Katt pulled the binocs out of the bin. He'd notched the plastic focus knob with his knife. In the dark, there was nothing to use to set the focus, and each lookout needed a different setting. He didn't tell anyone. He didn't want the focus knob on his binoculars filled with notches. Chief

Burns, with Sampson standing behind him, poked his head out the door of the pilothouse.

"See, Chief? Katt's on the job," Sampson said.

"Okay, Bosun. We're getting close to the *Yorktown*'s position. If she went down, the destroyers with her would have broken radio silence. So she's probably still on top of the waves. Keep your boys on their toes." The chief pulled back inside. "And I'm going to remind you, Sampson, the intel guys say we should expect Jap subs."

The ship slowed to twelve knots. *Let's go to work, Moriarity.* He wished he'd paid attention to all the chatter on the phone circuit. At any rate, the *Yorktown* was still afloat, maybe.

As he scanned his sector, he thought about how he had been so worried about dying himself at Pearl and at the Coral Sea. He'd seen those planes falling and spinning and burning, and he knew there was dying going on in them. The ones entombed in the *Arizona*. But they weren't Moriarity. Sometimes being on lookout meant a sailor had too much time to think.

He'd entered the navy for the paycheck. It wasn't much, but it was Daddy Warbucks rich to Momma. Once he got himself straight and started sending money, she wrote. The letter did sound like she felt rich.

The binoculars were just making the black blacker. There'd been black nights before, but none blacker than that night, or actually, early morning. Shortly after he saw the heart-lightening glow in the east, he detected a shadow about twenty degrees right. Look away. Look back. Big. Flattop. Katt reported it. Then he worked around the shadow. There were supposed to be destroyers too. One and then the other tin can solidified. They were so tiny close to the *Yorktown*.

From above him, a signalman flashed a brief message and got a couple of blinks in return from one of the smaller ships.

When he wasn't at his lookout station, Katt served as messenger, which meant he did whatever Boatswain Sampson needed doing. Generally, though, there was some time for standing at the rear of the pilothouse and listening. It was the way to get the word. The *Callahan* and the other two destroyers had a steady stream of flashing light messages going, the contents of which were verbally relayed to the officer of the deck.

The day before, on *Yorktown*, hours of efforts to contain fires in engine rooms were not succeeding. The list on the ship increased slowly but steadily. Before sundown, the crew was evacuated to cruisers and destroyers. Two destroyers were left to mark the final act in the life of the carrier. All night, the destroyer crews expected the *Yorktown* to plunge, but she floated all night, and, in the morning, the list was no worse than when the sun went down. A new plan was crafted: put damage control crews back aboard and rig the carrier for towing. The CO of the destroyer USS *Hermann* was the senior officer at the scene. He ordered the *Callahan* to a station northeast of the flattop and to screen the rescue effort from sub attack.

After hearing that message passed to the officer of the deck, Katt turned to Sampson, and using a church whisper, he asked, "One tin can screening a stationary target—can we do that?"

"Lot of ocean for a sub to hide in. But we got the job. 'Can do' is what we say," Sampson said.

Katt was back on the lookout station at 0740. The ship steamed back and forth across the northeast threat axis. Katt worked the binocs around northeast. A stick periscope? His heart kicked an extra thump. Look away and then through the binocs. Katt didn't know why looking away from the binocs for a moment helped him detect small objects better. It did, though. The tiny stick above the surface trailed the tiniest wake.

"Starboard lookout has a periscope bearing one five zero!" he shouted into the voice tube.

The general quarters alarm sounded, and the captain came onto the lookout station. The ship started a hard right turn and accelerated.

"Still got it?" the CO asked.

"No, sir. Once we steady up, I'll get him again."

"I bet you will."

The ship steadied. "Got him?"

Katt didn't answer for a moment. He looked away and looked back. "Got him."

"Will I be able to see him?"

"Well, pretty soon, sir."

Katt looked away and then through the binocs again.

"Torpedo! It's heading for the carrier!"

The captain brought his binocs up, stared for a moment, and barked into the voice tube, "Right full rudder. Break radio silence. Tell the other destroyers torpedo headed for the *Yorktown*." Then he grabbed Katt's arm and pulled him into the pilothouse. "Steady as she goes," the CO ordered the helmsman, and then he dragged Katt with him to the port lookout station.

"Two torpedo tracks now, sir," Katt said.

"I got 'em. The Jap was sneaking in for a close shot. We spooked him into firing long range," the CO said.

The captain made a small adjustment in the course. Then he watched the torpedo wakes through the glasses again and made another course adjustment.

Katt watched the CO studying the torpedo tracks. It dawned on him. He was going to have the *Callahan* eat the torps. Sacrifice a tin can to save a flattop.

Darn, Katt thought. *I didn't take out the government life insurance for Momma.*

Katt checked the torpedo tracks. He'd done it. The bow was going to catch one torp, and the other would hit amidships.

"Satisfactory, sir," Katt said to the captain's back.

He spun around. Katt saluted him. The captain stood straight and returned it. Then they both looked over the side. The torp tracks ran under the ship. The CO leaned on the bulwark, let out a breath, and slumped. He turned and faced Katt.

"Being alive's okay, sir. I mean, you look so disappointed," Katt said.

The captain coughed a couple of laughs from his belly.

"What happened, sir?" Katt asked. "Duds?"

"No," he said. "Sons of bitches set them to run deep. We only draw nine feet when we're light on fuel."

The captain ordered a hard left turn. "Let's kill a Jap sub," he said and clapped Katt on the arm. "Satisfactory, huh?"

Katt blushed as the ship heeled.

Behind the *Callahan*, a flash, a spout of water, an explosion. The *Hermann* lifted out of the water and broke in half, and the two pieces of her fell and went under. The *Yorktown* took another hit.

"Goddamn it, Katt," Sampson growled from behind him. "You can't help any of those people. But, you can help the *Callahan* by getting your head outta your ass and looking for Japs. Out there." Sampson pointed. "Where the torps came from. Not where the last ones went. Do your goddamned job."

Katt pushed the hundreds of sailors on the *Hermann*, the ones on the *Yorktown*, even Moriarity into a box to be dealt with later.

Find Japs, he told himself over and over. *Find Japs. Nothing else matters.* But other things did matter. *Find Japs.* He wiped his eyes with the back of his hand. *Find Japs.* He raised the binocs and searched for them. After a while, he didn't have to work so hard to keep the lid closed on that box in his head.

Two additional US Navy destroyers showed up. They joined the *Callahan* attacking the sub with depth charges. The *Spenser* picked up twenty-three survivors from the *Hermann*, and then she pulled her own two-dozen sailors off the carrier. The *Yorktown*'s list had increased noticeably.

All morning, the surface of the Pacific bulged with roiling ship-sized bubbles as the three destroyers executed coordinated depth-charge runs above where they hoped to see signs of Japanese death in the depths rise to the surface. At 1300, Katt picked up an oil slick, and the destroyers broke off the attacks and circled the wounded carrier, the flight deck now tilted at an extreme angle. Katt wondered why the big ship didn't tumble over.

Now, as the most senior officer present, the CO of the *Callahan* reported the situation via radio message. A reply ordered him to sink *Yorktown* with torpedoes and gunfire and return to Pearl Harbor. He acknowledged the message and reported he was ordering his ships to maintain radio silence. By flashing light, he determined the fuel states of the other destroyers. The *Callahan* and the *Spenser* were lowest but had a few gallons to spare. "Maintain circular patrol around the *Yorktown*," the *Callahan*'s signal lights instructed the subordinate destroyers.

At noon, Katt was relieved of his lookout duties. He ate and went to his berthing space for some sleep. Sleep would not come, however, and he pulled his clothes back on and returned to the bridge wing, to his post.

"What the hell you doing here?" Baldwin, the guy on watch, asked.

Katt shrugged.

"What the hell you doing here?" the boatswain mate of the watch asked.

Katt had to answer that one, but as he fumbled for what to say, the CO stood in the pilothouse doorway and told the boatswain to let Katt stay there.

"Aye, sir," the boatswain said, entering the pilothouse as the CO climbed up onto his chair.

"I guess that means you got the watch, Katt," Baldwin said, handing him the binoculars.

Katt started scanning for sub periscopes. Contentment settled through his chest and into his belly. He was where he wanted—maybe even needed—to be. Looking away from the binocs for a moment, he glanced at the profile of the CO sitting on his chair, staring straight ahead. Something had happened between him and the CO that morning. It was as if they'd become friends or something. And how could that be? A commanding officer of a destroyer befriending a seaman second, one who'd appeared at captain's mast and been punished?

Strange, he thought as he went back to work.

Through the afternoon and into the evening, the *Yorktown* floated. The list stabilized. Katt heard the CO tell the XO he couldn't order the sinking of the carrier. "I just can't," he'd said. They also discussed the idea of putting men back aboard the flattop to try to save her, but the CO decided the risk was too great, the probability of success too low. The *Spenser* hit critical fuel state for making Pearl. She was detached. The other three destroyers circled.

Just before Katt was due to be relieved of lookout watch at 2000, the CO came out onto the station and stood there staring at the outline of the carrier a half mile away. No moon. The overcast wasn't solid. Stars peeked through.

"Tough damned lady," the captain muttered, standing there silently for a long moment and then reentering the pilothouse.

A sailor walked out onto the platform and said, "Got anything to pass on, Katt? I'm ready to take the watch."

"I'm not leaving," Katt said. "You can stay if you want, or you can go back inside, and I'll man lookout. I'm not leaving."

"Well, shit. No sense two of us being out here."

Other than leaving the bridge wing for a few minutes to use the head and get chow, Katt stayed at his post.

Katt thought of the *Arizona* back in Pearl, the tops of her masts sticking up out of the water. Nautical tombstones. The *Yorktown* wouldn't have that. Who'd know about her, where she went down? Maybe Moriarity was on her someplace. Maybe he got off. Maybe he was already on the bottom.

At midnight, the junior officer of the deck came out and ordered Katt to go below and get some rest. The CO heard the conversation and told the JOOD to go back inside.

The CO and Katt stood next to each other, Katt doing his duties, the CO watching the *Yorktown*.

The overcast thickened. The night got blacker. Katt, as he did his looking, listened to the swishing of waves kissed aside by the bow and the hum of ventilation fans, as comforting to a sailor as a mother's heartbeat to an infant in the womb. Katt wondered if the *Yorktown* would cheat death again. Would sunrise find her still afloat?

A groan, obscenely loud, from the direction of the *Yorktown*, belched out of the dark and prickled his neck hairs. Some huge beast had just received a mortal spear stab. If he'd been dreaming, that's what he'd have thought. And the beast was angry. It wasn't ready to die. But he wasn't dreaming. The groan had not been that kind. It was … he didn't know what it was.

"I know, old girl," the captain said, barely above a whisper. "You fought good, but right now, it's just too much. I know."

A fresh groan troubled the dark water, and those watching saw nothing in the blackness. A small rattle, clatter, banging, and thumping grew louder and louder until it became a racket.

"She's rolling over," the CO whispered.

The explanation didn't make it any less spooky to Katt. Suddenly, the sound snuffed into silence, solemn and profound, like that morning in the Quonset hut church when it felt as if God might be there.

Out there, over the black water. Was He?

Katt heard the captain do a couple of short, sharp inhales.

Then from over the water came a *whoosh*, as if a large beast had died, its last breath driven out by collapsing lungs.

The captain slapped the top of the bulwark. "Shit," he said. Then he bent over the voice tube. "Officer of the deck, let's head for Pearl." He turned to Katt.

"We tried, son," the CO said, "but we came up short of satisfactory."

6

JUNE 8, 1942

As the *Callahan* snuggled up to the end of pier D1 at Pearl Harbor, the ship compressed the camel, a floating buffer between steel hull and concrete pilings. The camel emitted a living-beast groan. To Katt, it seemed for a moment as if his destroyer was telling pier D1 about the *Yorktown* rolling and plunging. Below him, the *Callahan*'s crewmen tossed mooring lines to sailors on the pier, and they muscled the thick lines—only a landlubber would call them *ropes*—to bollards. Katt unplugged his phone and wound the cord around the headset. Sampson stepped out of the pilothouse, leaned on the bulwark, and took in the activity below him.

"You know that commander down there staring up at us?" Sampson asked.

Katt looked. "Yeah. The day you guys tried to leave port without me, I was running to catch you, and he tried to stop me. He said he was the CO. I said he wasn't."

"Shit," Sampson said, pushing away from the bulwark. "I can tell by the look on his face he's an asshole." He shook his head. "I shouldn't be surprised. You never get two good COs in a row."

"That guy's going to be our new CO? Why do we need a new one?"

"We don't *need* one, but the asshole Bureau of Navigation sent us one anyway. But he won't be able to screw with us tonight. You going on liberty, Katt?"

"I want to find out what happened to Moriarity. Who should I ask?"

"I'll ask the division officer, see what he knows. But come over to the club later. I want to buy Eagle-Eye Katt a Primo." Sampson led the way down the outside ladder. He spoke over his shoulder. "Captain says you got Superman eyes. Anybody else reports something that the captain can't see, he doesn't believe it. 'Katt says he sees something, take it to the bank.' That's what the captain says."

Katt was stunned. He hadn't expected the CO to say anything like that about him. He'd convinced himself he'd imagined things, thinking the CO was his friend. That was crazy, he'd concluded. But now after what Sampson said, something had happened out there where the *Yorktown* sank. Something had happened to him. He was not the same person he'd been before. Maybe the CO had changed too.

At the main deck, Sampson went to find the division officer, and Katt had his own mission in the ship's admin office. There he asked for application forms for GLI, government life insurance. He'd stared death in the face, and not just once. To live up to the promise he'd made his mother, GLI was the thing to do. Taking the forms to the berthing space, he climbed up onto his bunk and began to fill them out. As he checked his entries, he made sure he'd put *n/a* in every space that was, for him, not applicable.

"Seaman Katt, you in here?"

A yeoman from the ship's office, Third Class Petty Officer Jasper, stood on the ladder, halfway down. The top of his head cleared the hatch, and Katt could see his face, the pointy wedge-shaped nose, the pursed lips. Moriarity said he looked like a weasel.

"I'm here," Katt said.

"Cap'n wants to see you."

"Me? What for?"

"I don't know what for. Get your ass in gear."

Katt rolled out of his bunk, being careful of the support for electrical cables just above him, and climbed down as the yeoman started back up the ladder.

"Jasper, hang on a minute," Katt said. "This is my application for GLI. Could you take it the ship's admin office—I mean, if you're going back there? Please?"

The third-class petty officer stopped and turned, disgust clear on his face. "Oh, sure, Seaman Second, since you're such good buddies, you and the captain."

Moriarity didn't like Jasper, Katt recalled. "You got business with the ship's office, see anyone but that guy," his friend had said. Too late. Jasper snatched the form out of Katt's hand.

"Thanks," Katt said.

Jasper mumbled, "Welcome, Seaman Second Shithead."

Katt decided to give it a week. Then he'd check with someone other than Jasper to see if his service record held a copy of the insurance application.

Usually, as he walked through the ship's passageways, he noted all the emergency equipment mounted to the bulkheads. Electrical cables for patching combat-damaged circuits, fire hoses, fire extinguishers, first aid kits, stretchers. Pumps for dewatering flooded spaces. If the Japs hit the *Callahan*, he wanted to know how to save his ship. But that day, he was worried about the summons. Ships' commanding officers did not summon seaman seconds to their cabins. It wasn't done.

Outside the captain's cabin, he raised his hand to knock, stopped, took a breath, and rapped.

An immediate "Enter" from inside stopped his hand in midknock. "Enter" came again. Katt jerked the door open, and the CO pointed to a chair. Katt asked, "You want me to sit down, sir?"

"Sit, goddamn—sit, please." The captain rubbed a hand over his face. He looked older than he had out there where the *Yorktown* sank. "I'm a little pressed for time, Seaman Katt."

Katt sat on the edge of the chair, and his right leg started jiggling.

The captain took a breath. "Okay, Seaman Second Katt. First thing. This paper promotes you to seaman first as of today. Congratulations."

Katt felt his jaw drop. He snapped it shut. "Cap'n—"

The captain held a hand up. "This paper"—the CO held up another document—"says you've been awarded two Navy Commendation Medals. Exemplary performance as a lookout—one for Coral Sea, the other for Midway. In a way, maybe your eyeballs should get the medals. But your brain drives those wondrous seeing instruments God put in your head. You deserve them."

"I heard medals take a long time, sir."

"They do sometimes." The captain looked down at his hands on the desk. "Okay, Seaman First," he said, looking

Katt in the eye, "as soon as we're done, go pack your seabag. This paper is orders." He handed that across the desk.

"I have to leave the *Callahan*, sir?"

"Yes, you do. You have a right to know why. You pissed off Lieutenant Commander Drake. As of about 1015 tomorrow, he will be CO of this ship. I know him. And I know you need to be someplace else. That's as much as I'll say."

"I don't want to leave the *Callahan*, sir. If he's mad at me, let him punish me. Don't make me leave."

"Seaman First, honest to God, I am pressed for time. I am doing not only what is best for you but what's best for our navy. You have to trust me. You have to go. Will you do that for me?"

Katt stood up abruptly and just as abruptly sat back down. "Cap'n, anything else, sir?"

The captain stood and saluted.

"Cap'n, don't. You're not supposed to do that."

"Yeah, yeah, I am." The captain dropped his salute. "You were next to me a couple of nights ago, just past midnight. You felt the *Yorktown* die. Same as I did. I was glad you were there when it happened."

Katt was having trouble keeping up with everything coming at him so fast. "Where are you going, Cap'n?"

"Frankly, I don't want to leave the *Callahan* either, but I have orders. I am getting a promotion and will command a squadron of destroyers."

"That's good, right, sir?"

The CO laughed. "Yeah, Seaman First, it's good. Now get the hell out of here."

Katt pulled the captain's door closed behind him and leaned against the bulkhead. "Shit," he said.

Why is it so hard to keep the no-cussing resolution?
Why does it hurt so bad to leave the Callahan*?*

He recalled being hungry and cold and afraid when he was growing up. Looking back on those problems, they all had a solution. Find food. Find a coat and gloves. Find a hiding place. Not that he found many solutions. *I've been cold before*, he told himself back then. *Tomorrow, I'll find a warm coat.*

Now the navy was taking his ship away from him. There was no solution for that tomorrow.

"You have to leave the *Callahan*. Will you do that for me?" the CO had asked.

He pushed himself off the bulkhead.

Down in the berthing area, Katt stuffed his uniforms into his seabag and snapped the hook through the top, sealing in all his worldly possessions. Sampson thundered down the ladder, and when their eyes met, Katt knew.

"Katt," he said.

"He's dead," Katt said.

"Yeah. There's confusion, but they have lists. There's a missing list, but the survive list and dead list are pretty sure. Moriarity's gone."

The boatswain put his hand on Katt's arm. "Sorry," Sampson said. Then his face went from somber to sunshine. "But I heard you got seaman first. Is that true?"

He knew Sampson was trying to cheer him up, pull him away from thinking about Moriarity. He didn't want to be cheered up. He'd thought they couldn't take anything else away from him. *But they can always find one more thing to take.*

"Hey, Katt. Did you hear me?"

He met Sampson's eyes and then looked away. "Cap'n promoted me," he said.

"What's with the seabag?"

"Cap'n threw me off the ship."

The boatswain rubbed his chin. "The new CO, Commander Drake. It have to do with him?"

Katt shrugged.

"Word is you also got two medals. That right?"

Again, the shrug.

"I'm buying Primos. Um, where you got orders to?"

"For right now, to the berthing barge at pier C."

"Okay, let's go," Sampson said. "Then we're getting knee-walking, commode-hugging drunk."

That's supposed to cheer me up? he thought. "Bosun—"

"Jesus Christ, Katt, lighten up. I'll watch out for you. I'll make sure you keep seaman first class longer than Moriarity did."

"I'm worried about you keeping boatswain's mate first class."

"You worry too much, Katt."

"Bosun," Katt began again.

"Now listen up, goddamn it. I am not leaving you alone tonight. Okay, I was kidding about getting drunk. We'll have one beer—or two maybe. Then we'll get a good dinner. So stop arguing."

Sampson ordered Wyatt to accompany Katt to the berthing barge to drop Katt's seabag off there and then to escort him to the enlisted club. "Or drag him if you have to," Sampson added.

On the quarterdeck of the *Callahan*, Katt's orders were signed by the officer of the deck. Then Katt saluted the ensign. It had never occurred to Katt before, but the American flag flying from the short staff at the stern in port and from the forward mast under way was called the ensign. As the American flag, the word *ensign* was steeped in respect. Ensign was also the rank of the most junior officer, and in that usage, it was steeped in disdain. In many ways, a seaman second was respected more than an ensign. *Funny*, Katt thought, *the stupid things you think of.* Officers and enlisted saluted the ensign when leaving the ship and when returning. Katt wouldn't be returning. *Ever.*

"Come on, Katt," Wyatt said, touching his arm. "I'll carry your seabag."

Katt shook his head, slung the strap of his seabag over his shoulder, and crossed the brow to the pier, and with Wyatt beside him, he set off down D1 and crossed in front of the head of piers D and C1 to where the berthing barge was moored at the head of pier C. On the trek, Wyatt again offered to carry the seabag or to help carry it, but Katt refused the offer. It wasn't just the weight of the seabag on his back, and the burden was his alone.

The quarterdeck of the berthing barge was on the bow. As he crossed the brow, Katt saluted aft, where he thought the ensign would be flying. Then he stepped onto the barge.

A third-class petty officer leaned on a plywood podium, reading a comic book. The guy smirked.

"Dipshit," the petty officer said. "This is a barge, not a commissioned ship. We don't fly no flag."

The petty officer took Katt's orders and then consulted a binder from a shelf under his podium.

THE HAPPY LIFE OF PRESTON KATT

"Bunk number two dash three dash four dash three is supposed to be empty. That's yours," the petty officer told Katt.

"You going to have someone show me where it is?" Katt asked.

"Dipshit." The petty officer sneered. "It's simple. First number means second deck. Then third row of bunks from the bow, and see, that's this end of the barge, case you didn't know."

"Hey," Wyatt said to the petty officer, "why you acting like an ass?"

"Let it go," Katt said to Wyatt, and to the petty officer, "Second deck, third row of bunks from the bow. What's the rest of it?"

The petty officer's eyes danced from Katt to Wyatt and back to Katt. "You don't sound like a boot."

"He's not," Wyatt said. "He's a seaman first."

"Yeah," the petty officer said, pointing to the stripes on Katt's sleeve. "That says he's a seaman second."

Katt grabbed Wyatt's arm and pulled him back a step. To the petty officer, he said, "Just give me the rest of it, the directions to my bunk." Katt repeated the deck and row numbers.

"Dash four. Count tiers of bunks from starboard side to port," the petty officer said. "The last number, dash three, that's third bunk from the bottom."

Katt repeated the sequence of numbers.

The petty officer nodded. "So go aft down either side," he said. "You'll find ladders going down." Then the petty officer went back to his comic book.

Katt followed the directions to the third deck and a

space filled with rows of tiers, each tier held a stack of bunks four high. He found his assigned bunk and hefted his seabag up onto it.

The space was lit with white light, another sign it was not a warship, that preserving night vision was not a necessity. Katt looked aft down the aisles between the tiers of bunks, a few of which were occupied with sleeping or reading sailors. Not one of those in the bunks looked out to see who walked past or claimed one of the few unoccupied bunks. The place was demoralizing and depressing. The place felt like the barracks that first night in boot camp. The place could just as well have been the surface of the moon, with Katt alone on it and seeing Earth so far away.

"Come on, Katt," Wyatt said. "Let's get to the enlisted club. Sampson's waiting for us."

Katt followed his friend out of the place.

Katt and Wyatt found Sampson, Molasses, and hulking Peterson at a table in the huge bar/dining area of the club crowded with tables arrayed in formation and occupied with sailors drinking beer and talking with loud voices competing with a general din. Sampson pulled out the empty chair next to him for Katt. Wyatt sat between Peterson and Molasses.

Sampson poured beer from a pitcher into cups and pushed them toward the latecomers. Sampson raised his cup. "To Moriarity," he said.

"Moriarity," everyone said.

Molasses raised his cup. "To the *Yawktan*," he said, and everyone aped the accent.

"To Captain Satisfactory," Peterson said.

"To Seaman First Katt," Wyatt said.

Katt picked his cup up. "To my ship," he said and drank.

The others echoed Katt's toast and drank.

The beer was cold, and Katt was thirsty.

Sampson told a Moriarity story. Katt had a second cup of beer. Molasses told a Moriarity story, and Wyatt went to the bar for another pitcher of Primo.

With all the cups topped off, Peterson said, "To Katt, one lucky bastard. Word is the new CO is a hell-on-wheels son of a bitch."

"Lucky bastard," the others said. Not Katt. He went into the head and sat on a commode. His head felt heavy … and numb. It was hard to think with the alcohol in there. He didn't pull his pants down. No business needed doing. Coming to the club with Sampson, he hadn't wanted to do that. He got swept along as he had with Moriarity. The beer, he'd guzzled it like water. Water went into a man's belly. Beer went into his head.

Katt stood and waited a moment for the dizziness to pass. Sampson and the others, they belonged to the *Callahan*. He no longer did. More beer was not going to lead to a good end.

Katt left by the back door and started walking toward the berthing barge. With each step, his legs behaved better. He wondered if he'd be able to find his bunk again in the dark. He remembered two dash three. The last number was three. He'd be able to find his bunk because his seabag was on it.

"Hope I can find the berthing barge," he muttered,

trudging along the dark street through the puddle of light under one pole lamp and aiming himself at the next one.

As he walked, thoughts pushed into his head: Leaving *Callahan* was God's punishment. The berthing barge was God's punishment. He'd sinned plenty after joining the navy and thought dying in a state of sin on December 7 was a sure thing. After confession and forgiveness, he gave up drinking, swearing, and rented women. But sins were mysterious things. They were all around, and they carried a Moriarity attractiveness. He'd drunk those beers with Sampson and the guys. He couldn't stop cussing. Maybe that's why he had to be punished.

By the time he walked from the enlisted club to pier C, he could think clearly. The second deck was all berthing, except for the head in the middle. He thought about the head as he descended the ladder to the third deck. On the *Callahan*, forty people used the head assigned to First Division. As soon as a sailor got to a sink to shave, the "hurry ups" began. Butt cheeks touched toilet seat. "Hurry up." Another as soon as the shower was turned on. After six months, it wasn't annoying anymore. Actually, it was amazing how quickly forty sailors finished their morning business. Morning on the berthing barge would be something. The barge had the same number of sinks, showers, and other fixtures as his destroyer had to serve four times as many people.

Now, though, the problem was to find his bunk. Dim white lights provided meager but sufficient illumination. He found the third row of bunks and started at the starboard side, moving to port looking for a seabag on the third bunk from the bottom. After crossing all the way to port without finding a bag, he retraced his steps, checking all the bunks from top to bottom in each tier. Several bunks were empty, but none had a seabag on it.

Maybe someone locked it up for him. Up on the main deck, Katt asked the petty officer on watch about his seabag.

"You left your seabag on your bunk, and you want to know if someone locked it up for you?" the petty officer, a different one but also a reader of comics, asked while leaning on his podium. "Someone stole it is what happened. You dumb shit. You don't leave anything lying around on the barge."

God's punishment, another one. He'd given up drinking but broken the vow at the club with Sampson.

The petty officer flipped a page. *Wonder Woman.* Those comics had just come out in the States. Sailors would give a month's pay for a dog-eared, wrinkled copy in Pearl. Katt tore his eyes away from the busty heroine before he sinned again, went back below, got undressed, and brought his uniform, shoes and socks, everything he owned, onto his bunk with him.

The next morning after reveille, the jam of sailors was much worse than on the *Callahan*. There, everyone pushed and shoved, intent on getting somewhere. On the berthing barge, no one shoved. No one cared if they made it to the head or not. Katt had no toiletries. He pulled his dirty clothes onto his sweaty body while lying on his bunk and climbed down into a pack of almost naked slugs smelling of beer sweat and sullen lethargy.

"Who's the senior petty officer in this space?" Katt asked a stubble-headed, thick-necked, slope-shouldered fireplug.

"Hell if I know."

The guy never focused on Katt. There wasn't much point in asking him anything else. The others either.

Katt made his way outside and forward to where another petty officer, another leaner, manned the lectern-like plywood box. Leaner wore white trousers and a T-shirt. He looked too old to be a seaman. So a petty officer.

Katt told Leaner his story. Leaner, still resting on an elbow, picked up a phone from the top of his box and dialed two numbers. "Silverman, 'nuther dipshit lost his seabag 'n' orders. Everthing." He hung up the phone. "The other side o' the barge. The second ladder up. Admin. Can't miss it."

"Thanks," Katt said, but to Leaner, Katt was already gone.

Admin was where it had been promised. Silverman was older than Leaner. Gray haired, round headed, and a soft man who worked indoors, Katt thought.

"So," Petty Officer Silverman said, "your service record, your health record, your pay record, all of them were in the seabag, right?"

"Yes."

Silverman sighed and handed a stack of forms to Katt. "Without a service record, you're dead. You don't exist. Fill these out, and we'll bring you back to life. Use that desk. You have to be out of here by 0730 though. That's when the others show up for work."

"Shouldn't we look for my seabag?"

"*We* aren't looking for anything. My advice? A search is a waste of time. Fill out the forms."

Katt filled out the forms and then went back to the place where the brow connected the barge to the pier. The place should have a name, but *quarterdeck* sure didn't fit. An officer of the deck manned a quarterdeck. The OOD represented the commanding officer. On the barge, there was none of the hierarchical orderliness that smacked you in the face from the moment you walked aboard a warship.

A younger leaner manned the unnamed place near the brow. Katt asked him about getting some help to look for his seabag.

"Won't do no good. Anything lyin' around gets snatched. Poof." He snapped his fingers.

With the loss of his seabag and records, Katt spent days reestablishing his US Navy identity. Getting a new health record was easy. A corpsman at the hospital pulled out a new folder and a new Record of Immunizations form. Since he had no proof of having his shots, he got them all again. He was sick for three days. God's punishment; some of it he was sure came from looking at Wonder Woman the way he had. *Nobody to blame but my own dad-burned self.*

At the Disbursing Office, a new pay record was started with his rank designated as E-3, seaman first. He was permitted to draw a salary advance to replace his uniforms. The service record was slightly more complicated. He explained the pertinent parts of his time in the service to Petty Officer Silverman: one captain's mast for being late, two Navy Commendation Medals for meritorious service as a lookout, and his promotion to seaman first. Silverman shook his head.

"Another bullshitter," Silverman said. "I get so tired of you guys making this crap up. I was beginning to like you."

Katt felt a streak of irritation flash through his head. Hadn't he suffered enough of God's punishment? But he knew getting angry at God, well, all that could do was earn more grief. Katt reached for that calm he'd experienced the morning in the Quonset hut church. Consciously, he drew in a deep breath, and then let it out. In. Out. It helped.

Silverman filled out appropriate pages in his record, designating Katt as a seaman second. He made no entry regarding medals but did include the captain's mast. Then Silverman sent Katt back to disbursing to get his pay record amended to E-2. The disbursing clerk informed him that he had drawn advanced pay as an E-3. Since he was an E-2, he owed the government a lot of money. Did he want to pay the money back in a lump sum? Katt had spent it all on his uniforms and toiletries, and he'd sent a ten-dollar money order to Momma.

"Son, you ain't gonna be getting much of a paycheck for a long time," the disbursing clerk told him with a bemused smile. Momma was getting a dose of God's punishment too.

Early every day, Katt visited the Quonset hut chapel. During the afternoons as he picked up cigarette butts around the base, he'd begun to think he had been punished enough. Before he entered the chapel, though, he pushed those thoughts out of his head. God's punishments were just. Katt had always gone to confession regularly, but the last time he'd been was the middle of December last year. He'd been wondering if the forgiveness made it too easy to repeat his sins. He didn't know if that was the case or not, but he worried that it might be. Just before he left the chapel, he always thought, *I am heartily sorry for having offended Thee.* There was another part of the Act of Contrition that went *because of Thy just punishments.* But Katt left that part off. The important consideration was that sin offended God, and that he needed to avoid offending Him for that reason and not to avoid being punished. So Katt had stopped going to confession. Forgiveness was not helping him to *sin no more*, which was another part of the prayer.

I am heartily sorry for having offended Thee.

Katt left the chapel and went to his next daily stop: Silverman's office. Silverman was the only authority on the barge. Katt convinced him to begin posting a twenty-four-hour security patrol on each deck of the barge.

"We don't do anything useful, anyway," Katt said.

Silverman agreed and revealed that until recently, sailors didn't stay aboard the barge long. There had been a lot of requirements for sailors on the battleships and ashore following December 7. Recently, the supply of recruits had caught up with demand.

"Also," Silverman said, "they're scraping some off the bottom of the barrel these days. Never seen such a bunch of criminals and misfits. A couple of these we've had sent back. Like yesterday. 'This guy is like having a Jap in our crew,' a chief told me after he'd been ordered by his CO to personally 'dump this sack of shit back where he came from.'"

"What ship was that?" Katt asked.

He rubbed his chin. "A cruiser, I think. The *Baton Rouge*, maybe. Yeah, the *Baton Rouge*."

"This was yesterday, you said?" Katt asked.

"Yesterday."

Katt told Silverman the cigarette-butt-picking-up detail could get along without him and that he was going to visit that cruiser.

He walked first to the end of pier D1. The *Callahan*

was tied to the end spot just as she'd been since Midway. A playful gust flipped the end of the black, rolled kerchief tied around his neck up into his face. It aggravated him. *Stupid kerchief. Serves no useful purpose.* He tugged his Dixie-cup hat on tighter. The lookout station, forty-two feet above the water. It tugged at him as if it missed him as much as he missed it.

7
JULY 1942

Compared to the destroyer USS *Callahan*, the cruiser USS *Baton Rouge* was huge—almost twice as long and almost twice as wide at the beam, sporting eight-inch guns versus the five-inchers on the tin can. Also, two brows connected the ship to pier A. The aftmost served enlisted men, while only officers used the forward one.

Seaman Second Katt stood on the pier looking up at the cruiser and took in not only the size of the ship but the steady flow of traffic on the after brow as well. Of course, a cruiser was much larger than a tin can. The crew had to be much bigger too. For a moment, he regretted that he was not a seaman first. The CO of the *Callahan* had promoted him, but then he'd lost his seabag, and Petty Officer Silverman had demoted him. A seaman first asked for a job, and his rank told of experience and seasoning. A seaman second's rank promised a wet-behind-the-ears boot needing a lot of experience and seasoning before he'd be worth much. A seaman second asking for such a job might get laughed at.

But, Seaman Second Katt, you've been laughed at before.

With his records under his left arm, Katt crossed the after brow and told a chief petty officer on watch what he wanted. The chief detailed a messenger to conduct Katt through a bewildering maze of ladders and passageways to the First Division office. Three desks jammed into the space hosted an ensign, a chief petty officer, and a yeoman third class.

"Chief Darwin," the messenger said through the door, "this seaman second wants to talk to the guy in charge of First Division."

The skinny, rosy-cheeked ensign looked up. He was about to say something when the chief growled, "Whatcha want, kid?"

"Heard you might be shorthanded, Chief," Katt said, twisting his Dixie cup.

"Pull that chair over. What's your name, where are you assigned, and why do want on the *Baton Rouge*?"

Katt told Chief Boatswain Mate Darwin his story. The chief flipped through Katt's thin service record.

"Your records got stolen, you say?"

"Yes, Chief."

"You had orders to leave your tin can. Why was that?"

Katt was worried about the truth. Silverman back on the barge thought he was BSing when he told him the straight story.

"Seaman Second Katt, you want on my ship, you give me the straight skinny. No bullshitting, or you can go right back where you came from."

Katt told him the story.

"Why would a tin can CO worry about a seaman second, especially one he had at captain's mast in November?"

"I don't rightly know, Chief. He was out on the lookout platform with me a couple of times. He was a good CO. I know that about him. I think he thought I was a good lookout."

"Good lookout." The ensign looked up from the papers on his desk and said to the chief, "We don't need lookouts. We have radar."

Katt watched the chief's jaw muscles work as if he were chewing nails. Both the ensign and the chief had close-cropped blond hair. The chief had a narrow forehead, the ensign, a broad one. Both had blue eyes. The ensign was slim. Hard muscle bulked the chief to almost twice the officer's frame. The chief stared at the ensign. He blushed and went back to his papers.

The chief turned away from the ensign and locked eyes with Katt. "Welcome aboard, shipmate."

The chief detailed Seaman Castro to show Katt around the ship and get him established in his berthing area.

"Big ship," Katt said. "I could get lost on here, and you guys wouldn't find me for a week."

"You get lost, nobody will come looking for you. So you'd best figure how to get to the mess deck."

After lunch on his new ship, Katt collected his new seabag from the barge and opened the door to Silverman's office and told him good-bye. Silverman gave him a limp-wrist wave but didn't look up from the papers on his desk.

On the *Baton Rouge,* Katt surprised himself by quickly learning routes to the mess deck, his morning muster station, his general quarters station, and the chapel. There were times when he had to stop and look at frame numbers and figure out if he was going forward or aft. The *Baton Rouge* was twice the size with twice the crew as the *Callahan.* The camaraderie he found in his First Division berthing space, though, was the same size as the one on his destroyer. And he liked having a chapel aboard where he could sit in the holy silence for a half hour.

There'd been no chapel on his destroyer. *His* destroyer. Funny, but that was how he looked at it. The *Callahan* and that vibration that made it impossible to see through binocs resting on the bulwark other than the way the CO showed him. He hoped things worked out for the CO in his new job.

On July 7, the *Baton Rouge* sailed from Pearl Harbor as part of a large task force sailing to the southwestern Pacific. After a month at sea, Chief Darwin sent a memo to the commanding officer via the First Division officer, the deck department officer, and the executive officer.

> Recommendation: Appoint Seaman Second Katt to one of the general quarters bridge wing lookouts. He is the eagle-eyed-est son of a bitch aboard.
>
> Very respectfully,
>
> Chief Darwin

In late August, the *Baton Rouge* was tasked with providing antiaircraft cover for the carrier *Saratoga* and to occupy a station one thousand yards abeam the flattop. The task force supported the marines who had gained a tenuous hold on a few square yards of jungle on Guadalcanal. Over two days, heavy Japanese air attacks concentrated on the carrier. Once again, Katt gazed at a sky splattered with black and gray puffs of burst antiaircraft shells, festooned with ribbons of tracer streaks, alive with falling, spinning, cartwheeling, dying planes trailing orange and red fire and black smoke. He'd seen it in the Coral Sea months earlier. And like at Coral Sea, the battle went on for days during daylight hours with desultory Japanese bomber raids at night. Throughout the attacks, Katt felt like a spectator rather than a contributor.

By the time the *Baton Rouge* had been at sea for seven weeks, supplies ran low. Replenishments would be scheduled, only to be canceled. Japanese subs sank some supply ships. The remainder diverted to support the marines ashore.

One of Katt's new shipmates, Olsen, said, "Good thing you're so damned skinny, Katt. Even the Spam is running low. Guys are talking about who'd be tastiest."

Then on the last day of August, the *Saratoga* took a torpedo.

"Word is," Olsen said, "the admiral thought the flattop was too vulnerable just sitting here locked to the jarheads ashore. *Sara*'s going home for repairs, and we get to escort her. Word is the jarheads are some kinda pissed at the admiral for pulling the aircraft carrier."

Olsen reminded Katt of Moriarity in some ways. He was always upbeat, and a person felt better after sitting next to him on the mess decks. He wasn't quite so brash, so prone to find trouble, and he was four or five inches taller and more muscled in the arms, chest, and neck than Moriarity. But he had the same facility for finding out what was going on.

Olsen continued, "After our float plane crashed, one of the guys from our aviation detail—Ashford, it was—got sent ashore with some spare parts the jarheads needed for their planes. He said the jarheads bitched at him the whole time he was there. 'Shithead no-load, fair-weather, sons-of-bitchin' squids,' they called us. 'Only took one shitty little torpedo,' they said. 'The carrier's still goddamned floating,' they said. Those jarheads sure talk dirty, ya know?"

Katt had been pleased to get back to sea, but he missed the *Callahan* and being so involved with the action. His destroyer would have been stationed farther away from the carrier where a lookout could see periscopes and torpedoes. If he'd been on his destroyer, if he'd been on watch, he was sure he'd have seen the *Saratoga's* torpedo. The CO would have … he didn't know what the new CO would've done. And he couldn't help feeling sympathy for the marines they were leaving behind with the fighting still going hot and heavy.

He wanted to go back to a destroyer. He wanted the *Callahan*, even with the new CO.

8

EARLY NOVEMBER 1942

In a month, the Pearl Harbor shipyard rendered *Sara* ready for sea. A task force formed around her, and she set sail again, with the *Baton Rouge*, for the Solomons.

Katt slipped comfortably into the routine of three section watches. One-third of the crew was at battle stations while the rest slept or worked. Katt fretted during nonwatch times when he cleaned, painted, and repaired boats and First Division gear stashed in lockers around the ship. He did his work, never needing a boot in the ass. But being at his lookout station was where he wanted to be. The Japs were sneaking up on them, hiding in the dark, hiding behind the clouds. That's what Japs did, and that's why God had given him his eyes—to find Japs. He hadn't found one, though, since Midway. It was a long time, and he wondered if his eyes had given out on him.

When the task force arrived in the Coral Sea, the *Baton Rouge* and two destroyers were ordered to duty around Guadalcanal. The Japanese were reinforcing their units by Tokyo Express, nightly supply runs by destroyers and submarines. The tonnage and number of reinforcements supplied each night was small, but the persistent effort was killing and wounding a lot of US Marines.

On the quartermaster's chart, Katt noted the gyrenes' position near Lunga Point. Also marked was the route the Japanese followed for their supply runs to a place called Tassafaronga.

"Word is," Olsen said, "Tokyo Express is runnin' tonight. 'Tween midnight and 0200, I heard." Seaman Olsen stood watch the same time as Katt.

Katt's heart thumped out a faster beat. He could feel Olsen was right.

As the sun was setting during Katt's 1600-to-2000 watch, the *Baton Rouge* took station astern another heavy cruiser, the *Macon*. From his lookout station, he saw other cruisers and several destroyers move behind the *Baton Rouge*, forming a battle line.

Katt's right leg twitched. When he was excited and seated, the leg jiggled quite often. Usually, it didn't happen while he was standing. He knew the enemy was out there in front of them, waiting for the dark and midnight, Seaman Olsen had said. The *Macon* wasn't going fast, fifteen knots maybe. Katt checked the sky with the last light. Overcast. It'd be a black one.

The sun set. As the last faint gray glow leaked out of the sky, the 2000 to 2400 relieved him. Katt hurried below and climbed onto his bunk. He slept soundly in half-hour stints, waking to check his watch. At midnight, he climbed out, dressed, hustled to the mess decks for a quick cup of coffee, and stomped up the ladders to his lookout station.

"What're you doin' here?" the on-watch lookout asked. The guy's name was Arnold. "You're not on till 0400."

"Can't sleep. You mind?"

"Nope. Just don't talk to me. Chief Darwin catches

lookouts talking, they get brand-new assholes to shit out of. I've grown attached to the one I got."

Katt had grabbed spare binoculars before coming out to the station. "Mind switching?"

The kid thought about it and finally said, "Hell if I care. Can't see anything with or without them. You want these, take 'em."

Katt found the notch he'd carved and set the focus knob. He began searching behind the lookout, with glasses, without glasses. Slow. Deliberate. Methodical. After thirty minutes, the on-watch lookout was relieved. Katt stayed.

At 0050, the smokestacks emitted a muffled roar. Down in the engine spaces, those huge machines had kicked into high gear. Through the hull, Katt felt the thrum of the propellers as they spun faster, chopping the water, grabbing for push, grabbing for speed. Ahead, the faint luminescence of the *Macon*'s wake widened. Katt smiled.

Soon, wind whistled past his ears. *Thirty knots*, he thought. Blackness all around. Blackness and Japs. The on-watch lookout was concentrating ahead. Katt searched to starboard, out to where he thought the horizon should be, and slowly worked his way forward.

Racing into total darkness, Katt had a momentary sense that the line of ships would hurtle off the edge of the earth, but the Japs hadn't fallen off the earth. They were out there.

The black night ripped open. A blinding light flashed from the *Macon*. Red-and-yellow flames fountained from her amidships. A muted *whoomp*—Katt thought it wasn't enough noise to accompany the explosion and flames—whispered past him. The *Macon* appeared to slam on brakes. A loud alarm sounded over the announcing system. It took a second, but Katt recognized it. Collision alarm. The stern of the *Macon* rushed toward the bow. The *Baton Rouge* turned hard left, barely missing the other ship.

Another bright flash, this one from the bow, port side. Another *whoomp*. A shock rammed through the hull and threw Katt and the lookout to the deck.

A ball of orange flames rose from the bow up into the sky and snuffed. A loud roar came from behind Katt. *Smokestack*, he thought, and he pushed himself up. A major portion of the bow was missing, including gun turret one. Turret two was still there, but flames licked up and around the barrels. A wave of heat washed back and singed his face. Then he saw the forward part of the bow, mostly submerged but still attached by steel sinew. The bow ripped loose and bumped and thumped down the side. A memory of the Jap sub inside Pearl Harbor interposed itself over the present for a moment.

Torpedoes. It had to be torpedoes.

I was on the wrong side. Before, he'd always been on the Jap side. For a moment, his mind stopped the earth and the battle.

Why'd You wake me, get me up here, and then let me be on the wrong side? Why'd You give me these eyes and put me on the wrong side? Why was I on the wrong side?

Guns on the ships behind Katt boomed sustained thunder. Katt looked aft and caught blink-of-an-eye glimpses of black water with liquid silver floating on it. When the destroyers fired, they made little booms, little flashes.

The *Baton Rouge* was slowing. The smokestacks roared. When the ship sailed fast, the boilers ran hot. If she slowed suddenly, the engineers had to vent excess steam out the stacks.

The *Macon* had drifted astern. Amidships, she was ablaze with a monstrous white-light bonfire and floating on a puddle of mercury. Katt wondered what happened to the color in the fire. He wondered if she would survive.

"Are we sinking?" The on-watch lookout was still on the deck.

"No," Katt said. "Not—"

The line of ships raced past to port and fired their big cruiser guns. Destroyers fired their little guns.

Chief Darwin charged onto the lookout station. "Who the hell's on the deck? Get up. Katt, come with me." The chief grabbed Katt's arm and dragged him through the pilothouse and out onto the port lookout station. "Japs're on this side. Don't let any of those bastards sneak up on us."

From the port lookout station, Katt could see wakes from the other US ships and the ships themselves for eye blinks in gun flashes. Fires burned on Guadalcanal.

Chief Darwin said, "The Japanese destroyers must have dumped their supplies and then shelled the marines near Lunga Point."

Katt saw a destroyer silhouetted against a fire ashore. The enemy. Katt had to think about the relative bearing on the port side before he reported it. Since Pearl Harbor, he'd always been on the starboard side.

The captain rushed out onto the lookout station.

"You still see it?"

"No, sir. Only saw him when he had fire on the shore behind him. Looked to be paralleling the coast, sir."

The captain scanned the shore with his binocs.

"You the eagle-eyed son of a bitch Chief Darwin told me about?"

"Um, sir—"

"Okay, Eagle-Eye. Do your stuff." He went back inside the pilothouse.

Katt worked the binoculars first, and then he worked his eyes over the area where the destroyers should have been. There had to be more than one. With the glasses on the bulwark, he peered through. There. He looked away and then back through. A destroyer and another. A third. Katt reported them.

The captain came back out.

"Where?"

"Just forward of the beam, sir. Three of 'em in a line."

"I don't see anything. You sure?"

Katt let out a breath and looked again. "Sure, sir."

"Captain," an officer said from the pilothouse, "the chief engineer says we should stop going ahead. He's worried about water pressure on the forward bulkhead. He's shored it up best he could. He says we should back to wherever you want to go."

"Back a third, Officer of the Deck."

"Aye, sir." The OOD issued the orders. Then the captain told the OOD to tell the operations officer to locate a spot where they could hide and effect repairs.

"Those destroyers, lookout?"

"I'm counting five of 'em now, sir. Still hugging the coast. Um—"

"What?"

"Lead ship's turning toward us."

"I can't see shit. Bearing?"

"Two seven five relative, sir."

"Navigator!" the captain hollered. "I need a range from present position to the coast on a two seven five relative bearing! And hop to it. Lookout, can you estimate how far off the beach the Japs are?"

"A thousand yards, maybe two thousand, sir. Not three though."

"Officer of the Deck, get the after turret trained on bearing two seven five relative. Gator, goddamn it! I need the range."

"Captain," Katt said. "The lead destroyer is continuing to turn. Could be reversing course."

"So he'll pass in front of those fires on the beach again?"

"Yes sir, couple of minutes yet though."

The captain shot the bearing angle to the fires through the alidade.

"Keep your eye on 'em, hear?"

"I got 'em, Cap'n. They're running away now."

"I told you to keep your eye on them. What're you doing?"

"Looking for periscopes. Might be a sub out here too."

"What's your name, sailor?"

"Katt, sir."

"Seaman Katt, keep up the good work."

The captain wanted to fire the after turret at the retreating Japanese destroyers. The chief engineer convinced him not to. "Fire the guns, and the vibration could dislodge shoring and mattresses we stuffed in holes to plug leaks. Ain't much keeping us afloat, Captain."

Katt had never heard a senior officer swear like the captain did. He wanted to fire his guns at the Japs. After scanning his side of the *Baton Rouge*, Katt noted three ships on fire behind them. They had to be American cruisers or destroyers. He'd seen no evidence that a single Japanese ship had been hit. What he'd seen of the Japanese force had been destroyers, and the Americans had cruisers.

The Japs still shot the crap out of us.

Head outta your ass, Katt. He was no longer on the *Callahan*, but Boatswain Sampson could still speak to him.

No one left his post through the night. Below decks, damage control crews patched holes ripped in the starboard side when the bow tumbled aft, reinforced the shoring at the forward bulkhead, and pumped water out of flooded spaces.

At his station, Katt watched for Japanese ships, but they didn't return. He didn't find periscopes or torpedo tracks either.

By morning, the *Baton Rouge* had backed into Tulagi Harbor, which the United States had captured from Japanese forces in August.

For the next eleven days, *Baton Rouge* sailors worked long hours and slept short ones. The captain's objective was to make the ship capable of a trip to a shipyard in Sydney, Australia. He sent sailors ashore to chop down trees and tow them out to the *Baton Rouge*. Logs were used for shoring and to bolster the forward bulkhead. The branches were spread over netting topside for camouflage.

During daylight hours, Katt was in the tree branches on the mast watching for planes. Below him, welders worked along the starboard side and on the bow. When Katt saw a plane, he wasted no time to determine friend or foe and called, "Knock it off," over a walkie-talkie. Welding ceased until he called, "All clear."

After eleven days, the ship was bandaged as well as it could be outside a shipyard, and she set sail for Sydney using reverse engines the entire way.

"You figure anyone's ever backed anything up—car, train, or boat—this far before?" Seaman Olsen asked.

Katt wasn't concerned with a world's record. He was concerned with having been on the wrong side of the ship. The starboard lookout station was his station. From there, he found Japs. But that night off Tassafaronga, he should have been on the port side. He'd known he had to be topside, to be at his station. Why didn't he know to go to the port side? He remembered the captain's attaboy, and he appreciated the CO saying what he did, but it didn't carry the weight of that one when he'd been on the *Callahan*. Still, the Japanese hadn't gotten all of the *Baton Rouge*.

That was something. It was hard work though, stretching *that* to cover the eleven days in Tulagi, the two weeks backing to Australia, the two and a half months of repair in Sydney.

From Sydney, with a stumpy makeshift bow that the cruiser sailors said shamed them, the long, slow transit to Hunter's Point Naval Shipyard depressed Katt more with each passing day. The Japs didn't get all of her. It was what he had, and it wasn't enough. Every day, the *Baton Rouge* carried him farther and farther away from ... some of the guys called them the enemy. "The enemy," to Katt, seemed not right somehow. He'd made promises: to the masts of the *Arizona* sticking above the harbor near Ford Island, to Moriarity and the *Yorktown* near Midway, to the *Hermann* near Midway, and now to 150 *Baton Rouge* sailors, including his buddies Castro and Arnold, at the bottom of the waters off Guadalcanal. Iron Bottom Sound, the guys called it. "We were lucky as hell," *Baton Rouge* sailors said. "We wound up with just the bow on the bottom."

Katt's promises had been very personal, made to specific sailors killed by very specific men, men with faces he saw in his mind. In his mind, he saw Jap faces. The Jap faces he saw were from the clips of newsreels spliced to the front of the movies they showed once in a while. In his mind, he saw Moriarity's face and faces of American sailors the Japs had killed.

Two days prior to the *Baton Rouge* arriving at a San Francisco shipyard, Katt sat alone in the chapel. The place was always empty of people at 1000, but it was filled with holy silence. Sitting on one of the dozen folding chairs, he could hear ship noises, but they came from another world, not the world of the chapel. Those noises could not affect the silence he felt and floated in. As he floated, there were no thoughts in his head. He felt his mind absorb wisps of the chapel's silence. He felt the burden of his promises lift off him.

Behind Katt, the door to the chapel opened and violated the silence. He spun around. An officer. A chaplain. The chaplain stopped in the doorway.

"Oh," he said. "I didn't mean to disturb you." He started to leave.

Katt hopped to his feet. "Wait, sir."

The chaplain stopped. "Is there something I can do for you, Seaman?"

"No, sir," Katt said. "I mean, well, this is more your place than mine."

The man had a nice smile. It was funny seeing an officer smile like that, even if he was a sky pilot. He took a seat across the aisle from Katt.

"I like to come in here and just sit in the silence," the chaplain said.

Katt almost said, "Me too," but he was afraid the chaplain might be the Catholic one and know he hadn't been to Mass.

"I'm Chaplain Fogarth," he offered.

He was the Catholic. "Um, the guys talk about you, sir."

"Yes, I know," he said, shaking his head.

"At Pearl, during the air raid, you said, 'Praise God, but keep passing the ammo.'"

"The guys believe that no matter how many times I tell them it wasn't me," Father Fogarth said. "Actually it was my friend Father Fogarty on the *New Orleans* who said that. I wish the guys would forget it. I don't care for the notoriety or to be remembered for someone else's deed. May I ask your name?"

"Katt, sir. Seaman second."

"Ah. Eagle-Eye. You are notorious also."

"You heard about me, sir? But I haven't done anything on the *Baton Rouge*. I haven't spotted a single Jap when it counted. At Guadalcanal, I was on the wrong side of the ship."

"Oh, I assure you, Seaman Katt, the guys talk about you." He looked at his hands for a moment. "I disturbed your quiet. I'm sorry."

The chaplain left. The silence had departed also. In the

dimly lit space, with unadorned painted metal bulkheads and mostly racks of cables overhead, only the excessively plain altar with the gold crucifix on it marked the space as a chapel.

Tears streamed down Katt's cheeks.

I was on the wrong side of the ship. I killed 150 Baton Rouge *sailors more than the Japs did.* Katt wiped the tears with the back of his left hand. With the right, he swept under his nose. Growing up back in Missouri, he'd learned there wasn't one thing to count on but his own guts. He didn't know who his dad was. Momma didn't know either. Or care. If he came in crying, she'd put her hands over her ears and holler, "Shut up!"

He swallowed his tears and ground his teeth for a moment. The cascade of anguished thoughts slowed, and returning calm slowly gnawed the distress from his soul.

9

APRIL 1943

Chief Darwin was on the lookout station with Katt when the *Baton Rouge* approached Hunters Point Naval Shipyard.

The chief said, "After backing all the way across the Pacific, I'm sure glad we entered port bow first. Backing in's a thing a ship could never live down."

Katt was bent over his binocs laid on the bulwark.

"Jesus Christ, Katt." The chief turned and looked at the Bay Bridge behind them. "Did you notice any of the sights coming in? The Golden Gate was under construction last time I was here. Bay Bridge too. Did you even notice Alcatraz and the city? Treasure Island wasn't built the last time I was here either."

The binocs were aimed at piers jammed with ships. The chief turned around and faced the bow.

"Jesus Christ, Katt. Look at the blue sky. Look at the United States of America."

"The *Callahan*, Chief. It's the *Callahan*."

"Where?"

Katt pointed. "Outboard destroyer in that nest of three."

"You still want to go back to her?"

"I do, Chief."

"I thought her CO had it in for you."

"Maybe he's gotten over it."

"We're going to be in the yards for more than a year. The Bureau of Naval Personnel is scraping up experienced sailors and sending them back to the war. You could get caught. They might send you to an oiler. So how about any tin can?"

Katt looked up at him. "I belong on a warship, Chief."

"Okay. I'll take care of it. You, however, have thirty days' leave. You're taking it."

"The last half of the alphabet was supposed to get leave first."

"Katt, I'm a chief petty officer in the United States goddamned Navy, and if I say *K* is in the second half of the alphabet, it by God is there."

Preston Katt tagged along with his buddy Harvey Olsen by hopping freight trains to Chicago. Then he hitchhiked to Saint Ambrose west of Saint Louis, Missouri. He climbed out of the stake-bed truck where Church Street crossed Highway 40, thanked the old-man driver, and closed the door. As his ride pulled away behind him, Katt took in the steeple of Holy Martyrs Catholic Church atop Church Hill. He recalled how high the walls stood, how the steeple rose to heaven. In third grade, when his teacher had been the nice nun, he thought he'd be able to climb the steeple to where he could step onto a cloud and climb a ladder right up to where Saint Peter manned the gate. When he recalled third, fourth, and fifth grades and Sister Ralph, he smiled.

In first and second grades, during recess, the other kids

pecked at him constantly as if he were the brood's runt chicken.

"Ragamuffin."

"You don't even know who your daddy is."

"Your momma's a drunk."

"Charity student."

"Runt."

All bleeding-word wounds he carried back into the classroom. He stuck with school because the abuse he received from his classmates wasn't as bad as what he received at home.

Then he moved to the third-, fourth-, and fifth-grade classroom and encountered Sister Ralph. She convinced parents to donate decent clothes for him. She made the boys include Preston in the noon recess game. He had no talent, but for three years, he played baseball.

Looking back on it, he saw his experience with Sister Ralph as a pivotal point. Prior to meeting her, his life had no more direction than a mongrel dog skulking around town searching for dinner. "We have souls," Sister Ralph said as she looked right at Preston. "That's the part of us that God loves. That's the really important part of ourselves." He still saw that day in fifth grade when she connected "Thou shalt not steal" with "By the sweat of your brow shall you eat bread."

Without the nice nun watching over him, his exclusion resumed in sixth grade, but he found another purpose. He began working with the custodian, removing cinders and stoking the furnace in winter, mowing the cemetery during the other seasons. No longer was he the charity student. That year, too, he delivered papers, the *Saint Louis Globe*

Democrat in the morning and the *Post Dispatch* in the evening.

Sister Ralph. If he hadn't met her, he couldn't imagine what his life would have become. He chided himself for not remembering her more often.

Preston picked up his zipper bag, which everyone called an AWOL bag, checked for traffic, and crossed the highway heading for downtown Saint Ambrose. Cornfields flanked both sides of the road for a few minutes of his walk. Then he came to a ball field on his right, and, on the left, a dirt levee, which shielded the town of Saint Ambrose from Verrückt Frau Creek during spring floods.

"*Verrückt frau*—what does it mean?" he'd asked Mrs. Grossman.

"Crazy woman. Crazy Woman Creek."

"Isn't that a funny name for a creek?" he'd asked. But Mrs. Grossman didn't want to talk about it further, which was funny. She was always easy to talk to.

The familiarity of the place where he'd grown up rode comfortably along on his recollection of his favorite teacher. He passed Grossman's Farm Implements and looked down Main Street. Two short blocks of businesses, two more of houses—Main Street, Saint Ambrose.

The other way, across the creek, the top of Momma's two-story wood-frame house stuck above the trees. A long time ago, Momma's house had been white. Now it stood alone, decrepit, ostracized to the far side of the creek by more comely structures in town.

The clock on the church steeple showed 3:00. Momma would be at work. She tended bedridden Agnes Fenstermacher from 11:00 a.m. until 5:00 p.m. It would be three years now that Momma had that job. He remembered Momma ate with Agnes. Most of the time growing up, there'd been no food in the house. He'd learned to fend for himself from early on. Sometimes the mothers of boys who taunted him fed him. Still, there had been a lot of hungry nights.

A block down Main and on the other side of the street, Grossman's General Store occupied the lower level of a two-story building. The family lived on the top floor. Mrs. Grossman ran the store, while her husband managed Grossman's Farm Implements, Grossman's Furniture, and the funeral parlor.

"Emil Grossman will sell you everything you need," a Saint Ambrose citizen would say, "from baby crib to coffin."

Another would say, "Every penny a man will earn his whole dad-burned life will wind up in Emil's pocket."

Which wasn't true. Townspeople spent money in Ollie's Tavern and farther down Main at the dented tin-siding, tin-roofed Treibmann's garage with its potholed, graveled-a-long-time-ago lot filled with cars, trucks, hay balers, combines, tractors, and bicycles needing fixing. Behind the garage and under a towering oak tree, Preston knew, was a weathered picnic table. Farmers and townsmen often brought a lunch box and beer from Ollie's and spent an entire day at the table drinking, eating, playing cards, talking about money-grubbing Emil Grossman, and checking on the Treibmann brothers every half hour. The brothers had a tremendous backlog of work. If a person showed up and stayed all day, he got his machine repaired.

Although everyone in town groused about Mr.

Grossman, no one said an unkind word about Mrs. Grossman. As men used Treibmann's and Ollie's to confess other people's sins, Sarah Grossman's store served the same purpose for Saint Ambrose women. Preston stood across the street from the general store. Through the big glass front windows, he saw Mrs. Grossman behind the counter with the cash register next to the door. She was speaking with two women—Mrs. Feldeman and Mrs. Ohlenschlager. For a moment, it was as if he was seeing Mrs. Grossman for the first time.

Her hair had always been a dark gray. *Huh. Navy gray*, he thought. Her round face, always kindly, always smiling. Again he chided himself for not thinking of her more often with gratitude. Every bit as much as Sister Ralph, Mrs. Grossman had helped put aim and purpose to his life.

He had worked for her through the last of his grade school years and all through high school. He rolled and rubber-banded his papers behind the store. He delivered mail and groceries and ran errands and did whatever she needed done. She wouldn't know how important she'd been to him. He wondered if she'd remember him after being gone for two years.

Preston crossed the street and opened the door. The bell jangled. The three women turned with identical expectant expressions on very different faces.

"Well!" Mrs. Grossman exclaimed. "As I live and breathe. Preston Katt." She bustled around the counter and took him by the shoulders, examining him as she might check a bolt of cloth for an imperfect weave. "I am majorly disappointed in you."

Preston's heart felt as if it stopped beating.

"I expected you to come home in your sailor suit." Mrs. Grossman shook her head. "The look on your face! I vas kidding. I make joke. You are best worker. I could not be disappointed in you."

She crushed him to her soft, barrel-shaped body. Over her shoulder, he saw the shock on the two women's faces as if the world wobbled. Katt pictured the women telling friends, "Sarah Grossman hugged the Katt boy. The Katt boy! Imagine."

"Boys go to var," Mrs. Grossman said. "Not come home."

Mrs. Feldeman's cloudy face brightened. The world steadied on its axis.

Mrs. Ohlenschlager said, "Oh my, yes. The Zoll brothers in Africa and Alfie Baum at Guada … Gwada … something."

"Canal," Mrs. Feldeman said. "Gwada Canal. Such places they send our boys to die."

Guadalcanal, from those women, gave Preston his own shock as he envisioned the black night, the torpedo explosion, the bow ripping away and bumping down the starboard side of the *Baton Rouge*, and 150 of his shipmates sinking to adorn the floor of Iron Bottom Sound. He dropped his AWOL bag.

"Ah! My bunion," Mrs. Grossman said, releasing Preston.

"I'm sorry, Mrs. Grossman."

He grabbed his bag, spun around, and headed for the door.

"I wanted to ask him," he heard Mrs. Ohlenschlager say, "if he knew that place. That Gwada Canal."

"Wait, Preston," Mrs. Grossman called. "I have something I have to tell you."

He didn't want to offend Mrs. Grossman, but he couldn't stay in the store with those women and their Gwada Canal. Groceries. He'd gone in for groceries. Going back was out of the question.

It wouldn't be the first hungry night he spent in Momma's house.

Preston crossed the bridge and turned onto the packed-dirt path leading through waist-high horseweeds and head-high willow saplings. The ground trembled. A train. Momma's house was as close to the tracks as those on Second Street. The train quake intensified, and he paused next to the front porch with the broken floorboards. The engine passed and *click-clack*s cadenced the rush of freight cars heading west. As he had when he was growing up, he wondered if the shaking would cause the tired, old, cadaver-gray, two-story wooden frame structure to tumble down. It was a long train. The house was still standing.

The house had been quite something in its day. Rumor had it Frank James moved across the state and built the place after the coward Robert Ford shot his brother Jesse. He'd asked Mrs. Grossman about the rumor.

"Ach," she'd said. "Half der towns in Missouri got a Frank James house."

The caboose rolled by. The trembling in the earth chased after the train.

He followed the three-foot-wide beaten path around the south side to the rear. Recalling how, in winter, when dark came early and dark was pitch blackness under the trees next to the house by the time he finished his evening paper deliveries, he'd slide his hand along the wall. At the rear corner of the house, he passed the pile of cans and bottles and moldering cardboard. Two large rats scurried away into the weeds.

Then he heard the voices.

"There's no goddamned whiskey," a man growled. "No goddamned gin. Put some clothes on and go see if that worthless shit sailor son of yours sent money."

"He sends money." It was Momma. "What do you do? Lie around here drunk."

There was a slap. Momma screamed.

"Yeah. You shouldn'ta quit your job with the cripple woman either." Another slap and scream. "There's not enough money coming from the boy."

The spade he'd used to dig worms leaned against the back of the house. Katt dropped his bag, grabbed the shovel, and charged through the door.

A man—a six-footer, gray, long-john bottoms, dirty undershirt—gripped Momma's upper arm, his other hand drawn back, ready to slap again. He glared over his shoulder. The guy's ugly grimace and soulless eyes stopped Preston.

"Preston!" Momma said as if she beheld a miracle.

The brute let her go.

Momma wore a slip and had ratty blonde hair. She rubbed her arm, and her sallow, sunken-cheek face lit with the cunning look he'd seen so many times before. "Musta cost money for you to come home. Why didn't you send me some? I need it. You have some left, don't you?"

Katt gripped the shovel. He didn't move, but his eyes did, dancing from one and quickly back to the other.

"Ozzie," she said.

Ozzie's face grew a smile, uglier than the grimace. He lunged forward, arms about to grab the skinny kid when Preston jabbed the shovel handle into the man's gut. The soulless predator eyes flooded with pain and panic. Ozzie howled, clutched his belly, and fell onto the floor.

"Ozzie." Momma bent over him.

Katt dropped the spade. It clattered on the warped wooden floor. Momma tried to get Ozzie upright. He moaned and fell back.

Katt looked back through the open door. Momma jerked at Ozzie's arm, but he had both wrapped over his belly as he rocked with his eyes shut tight.

"Get up, Ozzie. He's getting away."

Katt turned his back to them, to the house, his chin sagged onto his chest. For a moment, he didn't care if Ozzie grabbed him and beat the crap out of him. But the man's moaning was all that came out the door. Katt lifted his chin and headed for the highway, the westbound side.

There he looked up at the church steeple and thought about Sister Ralph. After a moment, he turned and spotted the top of Grossman's General Store. A fond thought for Sarah Grossman wafted through his mind. He turned a little to his left to where the house of Frank James sat hidden by the trees along the creek. He thought of the box in his head where he stored things to be dealt with later. He had a new box up there, he decided. He buried Momma in that box.

10

END OF APRIL 1943

K att found the *Baton Rouge* sitting on blocks in a dry dock. After changing into his uniform, he reported to Chief Darwin.

"What the hell are you doing here, Katt?" the chief asked. "You still have two weeks of leave. Didn't you like being home?"

"Home's here, Chief."

The chief glanced down at his hands for a moment. "It's good to see ya, you little shit," he said.

Katt blushed, and emotion erupted out of his belly and lumped in his throat.

"Well, hells bells," the chief said. "I just remembered. USS *Dalton* is scrambling a crew together. Bureau of Naval Personnel took a bunch of sailors because she was going in the shipyard for overhaul, but that was delayed. They get under way tomorrow. You interested?"

"You know where they're going?"

"Course not. You interested?"

Katt nodded.

"One more thing. You're out of uniform."

Puzzled, Katt began looking himself over. He checked his fly.

The chief laughed. "Your promotion came in. Effective date of a year ago. You know what that means?"

The seaman first shook his head.

"Most guys would have asked about back pay." The chief laughed again. "There will be that, but what I meant was you can take the test for third class next month. Petty Officer Katt! Jesus Christ! What the hell is my navy coming to?"

The *Dalton* was the same class as the *Callahan*. After the lookout post on the cruiser, the cramped station sited closer to the ocean surface felt like home to Seaman First Katt. What didn't feel like home was the frigid northern Pacific.

Seaman Second Morrisey the Mouth said, quite often, "Sweating your balls off in the south is a lot better'n freezin' your ass off in the north."

The other thing that did not feel like home was how the *Dalton* rolled in the unrelenting heavy seas and high winds. On the *Callahan*, there was always the feel the ship would right herself, even in high-angle rolls. On his new ship, Katt had the feeling quite often that even a relatively small roll would continue to a capsizing. Eventually, though, the destroyer would come to an understanding with the sea and behave like a proper ship, for a moment or two.

The *Dalton*'s leading First Division petty officer, Boatswain Abel Zwick, told Katt, "The navy stuck a radar on us the first of the year. Made us top heavy. We roll different from before. You'll get used to it."

Katt didn't get used to it. As the *Dalton* steamed back and forth screening the amphibious ships invading

Kiska in the Aleutians, all the forces of nature seemed to conspire against a lookout. He couldn't rest binoculars against the bulwark because of all the jerky gyrations. The wind and the cold tore at his cap, penetrated his foul-weather gear, numbed his fingers and face, and froze his toes. The wind also ripped the tops off the waves and filled the air with spray. Seeing a periscope would be hard, even for him.

"It's shitty out," Boatswain Zwick told the lookouts. "For the Jap subs too. The little yellow bastards, if they're out there, are banging around inside the sewer pipes like marbles in a tin can. But ... but, those little yellow bastards are tough. Question is, who's toughest?"

I am tougher'n the Japs.

Katt gritted his teeth and fought the elements. After a time, the wind howling around the superstructure and rattling signal flag halyards like a bunch of kids beating on buckets with mixing spoons, the numbing cold, and the spastic motions of the ship wore him down. He began to long for the end of his watch, which he'd never done before. Then he remembered to pray. Praying made a world of difference.

After a week of being tossed about by the northern Pacific swells and winds, the amphibious invasion of Kiska was completed. Katt took it as an answer to his prayer. The assaulting soldiers must have prayed too. Their landing had been unopposed.

"Except by two yellow, slant-eyed dogs," Mouth Morrisey said. "When the first boatful of soldiers waded ashore, them two dogs came running down the beach barking like crazy. '*Alf, alf, alf,*' they went. A guy raised his

M1 to hose 'em. A sergeant stopped him. 'The captain wants prisoners to interrogate,' the sergeant said."

Lots of the guys laughed. Katt didn't. Nothing about Japs was funny.

At least they were headed for Hawaii. After the operation, the *Dalton* escorted the amphibious convoy to Pearl Harbor and warm weather. Katt hoped they'd go on to the western Pacific and the war, but he was disappointed. The *Dalton* set sail for San Francisco as part of a convoy of naval support vessels on the way to West Coast shipyards for overhaul. Following that, *Dalton* made two more laps of the Aleutians to Pearl Harbor to the West Coast circuit, escorting various task groups on various missions, and then she was ordered to the Hunter's Point shipyard to complete her overhaul. Upon arrival in the yard, Katt asked for a transfer.

"Not going to happen," Boatswain Zwick said. "They're transferring me to the *West Virginia*. They finally got her fixed up after the Japs ripped the guts out of her at Pearl. You just made third class petty officer, and you gotta stay and supervise the crew in the shipyard."

The *Dalton* wasn't scheduled to complete the overhaul until the early part of 1944. Katt was demoralized. After having been in on all the big naval battles in the Pacific in 1942, 1943 had been a bust. He'd spent weeks in the first part of the year backing away from the war. In the end, all he had done during the second full year of war was to participate in the capture of two Jap dogs.

11

JANUARY 1944

Finally, the end of the long overhaul period was in sight. That day, the shipyard would flood the dry dock holding USS *Dalton*. On the berthing barge adjacent to the dry dock, reveille sounded. Sailors rolled out of their racks and hustled to the head, pushing to get to one of the six sinks.

Seaman Second Morrisey the Mouth at one of the middle sinks had no trouble shaving and talking at the same time. "It's Tuesday. At least the goddamned navy didn't try to float our boat on a Monday. Who'da figured they had so much sense? And! And have I told you guys this is an even more auspicious occasion?"

"Shaddup!"

"We heard it already."

Five foot nine, 130-pound Morrisey was not deterred.

"Yesterday was my last day of restriction."

Two months prior, Morrisey had been promoted to seaman first. He hosted a prodigious celebration in a bar outside the shipyard gate. The next morning, he appeared at captain's mast dressed in blues and two black eyes. For being drunk and disorderly, destroying civilian property, and assaulting a shore patrol petty officer, he was reduced in rank, fined, and restricted for two months to the berthing barge and working on the ship. Now the restriction was over.

"Celebration tonight," Morrisey said. "At O'Malleys."

"No," Petty Officer Third Class Katt said from an end sink. "You have duty tonight, Mouth."

"Jesus Christ, Katt. Give me a break. I been on restriction for sixty days."

"It's Petty Officer Katt. Duty tonight. Give me any more crap, and you'll get duty tomorrow too."

Katt exited the head as Mouth mumbled "shits" at the polished aluminum mirror. Katt's bunk was forward, but he heard shouts from aft. Near the rear of the compartment, he saw a crowd of guys restraining hulking Quinn. It appeared Quinn wanted to get at the colored kid Mattson. Katt hustled aft, his shower shoes flap-flapping.

"What's going on here?" Katt demanded.

The crowd around Quinn parted. He pointed at Mattson.

"This *nigguh* accused me a stealing!"

Mattson worked hard. Quinn worked hard at avoiding work and fomenting trouble. "Did you?" Katt asked.

"You takin' the word of a—" Quinn bellowed, shaking the guys off his arms and charging.

Katt's head emptied of thought and filled with cold calm. He waited, Dopp kit in his right hand. Quinn, growling, reached meaty paws to grab him. Katt ducked, jabbed a forefinger into Quinn's eye, and stepped aside as the big man charged past and into the corner of a locker, ripping it from the deck. Quinn wound up on his back next to the locker. A cut in his forehead leaked blood. His bare chest rose and fell.

Breathing.

"Darn," Katt said. "Ruined my shower shoes." He found Andrews in the crowd. Andrews was Quinn's buddy. "Andrews, go up to the duty petty officer post. Tell the PO Quinn tripped and hurt himself. He's unconscious and bleeding." Katt pointed at Andrews. "Tell him just like I said it."

Andrews squeezed past Katt and the injured man. Katt picked up the towel and tied it around his waist again.

"So, Mattson. He stole something from you?"

"I think he did, Petty Officer Katt. He didn't like I axed him about it."

"What got stolen?"

"A gold cross. He told me last night, a ... I shouldn't be allowed to own something like that. This morning, I found the chain was cut while I slept. The cross was missing."

Katt pulled the beaded chain with his keys and dog tags from his neck and held them out to one of the sailors. "Eckels, this key opens the locker with the bolt cutter. Get it and bring it here." To another, he said, "Wilson, get a towel and hold it against Quinn's forehead to stop the blood."

After the bolt cutter arrived, Katt cut Quinn's lock and pulled a cross out of the personal items drawer at the bottom of the locker.

"This it?"

Mattson said it was. A sound cloud of angry murmurs filled the space. Sailors hated thieves. "More than the goddamned Japs," one clear voice said.

Quinn groaned. "Oh, Jesus, my head. Ow, goddamn! My eye." He started to get up, and two guys grabbed his arms to hold him down. That enraged him, and he thrashed his arms and pushed the hands away and himself up.

"He wants to stand up, let him," Katt said. "Don't let him hurt any of you."

The beefy man swayed on his feet like a huge trunk-chopped tree deciding which way to fall. He puked and fell into the puddle.

Andrews returned.

"Well?" Katt asked.

"I told the petty officer of the watch like you said. He called an ambulance."

Quinn's upper body twitched. He raised a hand to his right eye. His left was scrunched shut.

"Okay, Andrews. Stay with your buddy. The rest of you, get on with your business. Seaman Mattson, come with me."

Halfway to the head from where Quinn lay, Katt stopped.

"Mattson, I pulled you out of the galley because I saw how hard you worked. I didn't mean to make trouble for you with the likes of him." Katt hooked a thumb behind them. "I know he's not the only one."

"No, Petty Officer Katt. Not the only one. Just the worst. An' I ain't got no beef with you."

Katt placed his aluminum tray on the table occupied by his buddy Petty Officer Young. Young was a third-class radar technician.

"So, Katt," Young said. "You put Quinn down this morning."

"Word gets around fast."

"Sure, something like this. 'You hear what happened? Katt floored that big-assed Quinn. Yeah, Katt. Weighs just over a hundred, soakin' wet. Put the gorilla down, he did.' That's the word." Young grinned at Katt. "So, Katt, that stuff I taught you in the gym, it worked?"

"You sound surprised."

"I had no idea it would work in a real fight."

"Really?"

"Yeah. I've been practicing it since second year of high school, but I was never in a fight."

"I remembered what you told me about fighting a big guy. 'You got to hurt him fast and seriously. You got to attack vulnerable spots: eyes, throat, balls, gut, knee, chest.' The way it went down, there wasn't time to think beyond the first item on the list of vulnerable spots."

"When we did the last slap-to-the-face drills, you showed me fast hands, good reflexes, and most important, cool. You didn't get hot when I slapped you a couple of times, which happens to most people. Me fighting Quinn, I'm not sure I'd have been cool. While I was peeing my pants, he'd have ripped my head off."

"Then the CO would've hauled Quinn in front of a firing squad. Only two of you aboard can fix the radar. And everybody knows it needs lotsa fixin'."

USS *Dalton* spent a month escorting new and repaired ships from the West Coast of the United States to Pearl Harbor and escorting battle-damaged ships back to the United States for repairs. Then, after Katt had bellyached to Young about never getting back to the war, the ship was assigned screen duties for three new jeep carriers on their way to participate in the invasion of Saipan. After arriving in the Marianas, the jeep carriers were assigned to the task forces assembled there. The *Dalton* spent a night providing five-inch covering gunfire for the underwater demolition team swimmers reconnoitering landing beaches and clearing obstacles.

The next morning at breakfast with the bombardment still under way, after a *wham* hammered through the hull, Young said to Katt, "Ah, the smell of gun smoke and bacon in the morning."

"You're pretty chipper for so early," Katt said.

"Yeah. The CO let me pull the vacuum tubes out of the radar before we started firing the guns. We don't have many spares left."

Katt paused, a forkful of scrambled eggs halfway to his mouth, and then he dropped the fork onto his tray. Katt felt like an old man. Young knew things and thought of things that could never have entered Katt's mind as original thoughts.

"What?" Young asked. "Why are you looking at me like that?"

"The things you know," Katt said.

"*Puh!* The things you know are worth more to the navy than what I know. My radar is broke more than it works. You, the guys still talk about your fight with Quinn. And Quinn gets bigger each telling."

"That was eight months ago."

"Yeah. But they talk. 'Quinn charged. Katt's towel fell, and he stood there buck naked, his dong hanging down, and he was still a goddamned petty officer in the United States goddamned Navy.' That's what they say."

"*Puh*," Katt said.

The *Dalton* was busy in October with shore bombardment, escort, and task force screening assignments while Marianas operations wrapped up and the invasion of the Philippines began. The second week in November, the ship received a new assignment.

"Forward radar picket, the navy calls it," Mouth Morrisey said. "Kamikaze magnet, I call it."

"Mouth is right," everyone agreed. The ship had never been alone, a hundred miles away from the heavies in the direction of the enemy before.

"We're not really alone," a sailor pointed out.

"With another puny-assed destroyer and a punier-assed destroyer escort, we are alone, man," Mouth said. "We oughta have a coupla battlewagons, some cruisers, and ten more destroyers where we're going."

"Well, the thing I heard," another sailor said, "that destroyer escort has special radar for finding Jap planes."

"See, dipshit," Mouth said, "the important thing is we got nothing much to protect us after we find the Japs. And if we find them, they sure as shit will find us."

The next morning, dawn gave way to a sky empty of clouds and unlimited visibility except for a band of white haze on the eastern horizon. Katt, the boatswain mate of the watch, was on the starboard bridge wing checking on the lookout, Mouth Morrisey, when the big orange-red sun burned through the haze.

"Oh, shit. Look at that, Bosun. It's just like the red meatball painted on Jap planes."

"It's the sun, Mouth. It comes up every morning. Get those binocs working. Periscopes and planes."

"That meatball sun, bad juju, I'm saying."

"Mouth, one more word, and you're on permanent head-cleaning detail."

Katt stepped back inside the pilothouse, and he heard Mouth mumble obscene *-ing* words along with his name. He shook his head. Mouth was okay if he was out of earshot.

A signal light began blinking on the destroyer escort USS *Edison.*

"Bridge, this is signals, *Edison* reports multiple air contacts bearing three zero zero. *Callahan* orders battle stations and to close in to five hundred yards on *Edison.*"

To Katt, steaming with his old ship was not as good as being on her, but next best, and it seemed appropriate that the *Callahan* had the senior captain. The purpose behind the order to close on the destroyer escort wasn't hard to figure out. The DE had long-range air-search radar, and the *Callahan* and the *Dalton* had more firepower. The two larger destroyers had to protect the little one and its radar.

The First Division senior petty officer took over as boatswain mate of the watch, and Katt relieved Mouth as the starboard lookout. He'd been a petty officer for ten months, but starboard lookout was where he belonged. After searching forward with the binoculars, he scanned the sector with his eyes. In the guntub a deck below and forward, Seaman Mattson grinned up at him and gave him a thumbs-up. Mattson was a loader on the pom-pom twenty millimeter. Katt returned the gesture.

Resuming his scan, Katt checked for periscopes ahead and then for planes out on bearing zero four five relative to the bow. He saw dots. He took his eyes away from the glasses, blinked, and looked again. He saw dots. Planes. Japs.

He yelled into the voice tube, "Starboard lookout has ten air contacts! Zero four five relative! Elevation angle twenty!"

Katt kept the binocs on the planes as he waited for something to happen, but nothing did. Maybe they hadn't heard him. He reached for the lever to open the pilothouse door, intending to repeat his report, when the smokestack growled, accelerating propeller vibration thrummed through the hull, and the ship turned hard left. The other two ships followed the *Dalton*'s turn.

The five-inch mounts and the pom-pom slewed and elevated their barrels. Katt scanned the rest of the sky, searching for more planes. Then as he scanned the surface for periscopes, the ship steadied with the air contacts on the beam. No periscopes, but three of the Jap planes pushed over into a steep dive. All three five-inch mounts fired as one—*wham* accompanied by a steady *pom-pom-pom*. The *Dalton* heeled as the ship turned hard right, along with the *Callahan* and the *Edison*.

The three Jap planes dove through a pipe filled with black puffs of shell bursts and pom-pom tracers. One plane lost a wing and spun violently, shedding parts. Another disappeared in a flash. The *Dalton* abruptly reversed her turn and threw Katt against the bulwark. The *Edison* had drifted astern. Her top speed was several knots slower than regular destroyers. Katt watched as the third plane bore in on the *Edison*. He was sure the Jap was going to crash into the radar ship, but it crashed just behind it. A huge explosion lifted the stern of the *Edison* out of the water. The bow dug into the sea, and for a moment, Katt thought the ship would dive to the bottom, but it sank to the level of the pilothouse and then bobbed to the surface, throwing off tons of water. But the *Edison* stopped dead.

The Callahan turned hard right, heading back to the stricken radar ship. The *Dalton* followed. The sky was now streaked with trails of black smoke. The gunners had knocked some of the attackers out of the sky. Katt saw a piece of a Jap plane crash onto the after five-inch mount of *Callahan*. There was a puff of smoke, and the gun barrel blew out of the mount, but the destroyer didn't slow down.

Katt checked to see how *Edison* was doing, but the ocean back there was empty.

Lookout, look out. That's what Boatswain Sampson told him at Midway.

Amid all the visual trash in the sky, Katt picked up a plane as it pushed over into a dive.

"Plane diving on us from dead ahead, elevation angle forty!" Katt shouted into the tube. The forward gun barrels stopped firing to the side, swiveled forward, and elevated. Then they began barking again, *wham-wham* and *pom-pom-pom*. The tracers came close. The shells burst close, but the Jap plane flew through. It had them nailed.

For an instant, everything stopped. There was no sound, no feel, no smell, only the plane hanging in the sky, a curl of vapor from a wingtip, a glint of silver sunlight from the prop.

God, don't let me be killed by a Jap. Please.

A ball of white light. A sense of floating. The ball of light collapsing in on itself. Blackness.

12

DECEMBER 1944

Katt opened his eyes and immediately slammed them shut. Light hurt. He moaned. His moan sounded funny, as if it came from the bottom of a well.

He heard, "The rest of these going to make it, Doc?"

"Damned if I know, XO." Katt recognized the voice. First Class Hospital Corpsman Duffy from the *Callahan*. "Those three burn victims from the *Dalton* … but my two amputees, if I can get some transfusions going, they'll hang on for a while."

"We're making thirty knots. It'll take us three hours to get back to Leyte Gulf, probably another hour to transfer the guys to the hospital ship."

"It depends more on how tough these guys are than on me, XO."

Katt opened his eyes a crack and winced. But he knew where he was. He was in the wardroom on the *Callahan*. He'd been there a number of times. When he'd been a seaman second, he was always a casualty during battle drills. The littlest guys always played casualties. Part of the drills was to carry the wounded to the wardroom, which served as the triage and hospital during battle stations. He started to push himself up.

"Whoa there, buddy." A sailor wearing a bloody T-shirt held him by the shoulders. "You ain't going anywhere till Doc checks you over, and he's busy right now. Lie back. Just lie there, quiet like." The kid went back to the table to help Doc. Enlisted man Doc Duffy was not a doctor, of course, but the sailors called him that. At times like then, being in the care of a doc was comforting.

A man in khakis, a lieutenant, walked past Katt and out the door.

Looking under the table, Katt saw a man lying on a mattress. A bloody mess of gauze was where his knee should have been. A red tube was stuck into his arm. The tube ran down from the wardroom table where another man lay. Blood donor.

Lifting his head and peering between his feet, he saw another sailor on a mattress.

"That you, Mouth?" Katt asked.

He didn't answer.

"*Dalton*," Katt said. "What happened to her, Mouth?"

"Gone." That was all Mouth had to say.

Katt watched Doc pull the needles from the two men.

"Mouth?"

"Yeah?"

"How'd I get here?"

It was quiet for a moment. Katt thought he wasn't going to answer.

"Mattson and me," Mouth said, "Just before the plane hit, we jumped. After the explosion, you came flying through the air and landed close to us. You'd lost your Mae West. We grabbed you. Then we watched the *Callahan* hauling ass away from us, forward guns blazing. Finally, the shooting stopped. She was a long ways away. There were sixteen of us in the water. All from the forward part of the ship. We didn't think she was coming back for us."

"Unger," Doc said to his bloody T-shirt assistant, "I think everybody here is as good as I can make them. I need to check on the guys in sick bay. Minor stuff, the XO said, but I gotta check. You need me, call."

"Aye, Doc."

Doc left, and Unger circled the table, checking on the guys on mattresses ringing the room. Nobody moaned. Nobody made a sound, except for Unger as he stepped around the wounded.

"The *Callahan* came back," Katt said.

It took a moment, but Mouth picked up the story. "She pulled right up to us. Pretty soon, all along the length of the ship, they were hauling guys out of the water. We got a line around you, and they pulled you aboard. Then me. I had a cut on my forehead where a piece of plane or ship hit me. They got a line to Mattson, but a shark pulled him under."

Mouth was quiet. Katt saw Unger sitting on the table staring at Mouth.

"I was bleeding," Mouth said. "My blood attracted that damned shark, but it got Mattson."

Unger was about to go to Mouth, but Katt signaled him to stay.

"Jesus goddamned Christ, Mouth, you can't put that on yourself."

The sentence came out of Katt's mouth as if someone else spoke it. *I'm alive, and Mattson is dead.* Morrisey was still alive, and he needed help.

"Jesus goddamned Christ, Mouth! You got the most

important thing done. You saved one of the navy's highly valuable third-class petty officers, me, so that the war against the Japs can go on. That's all that matters."

"What? You son of a—" Then Mouth started laughing. Then he cried. Then he laughed some more.

I'm sorry, God, about the cussing. I didn't know what else to do for Morrisey.

Then it sank in. He was back on the *Callahan*.

But two ships were lost. Two crews lost. Blown up, drowned, burned, eaten by sharks.

I don't think I can carry any more deaths, God, he thought and fell asleep.

A noise woke him. Under the table, Katt saw Doc Duffy and Unger load the man with the missing leg onto a stretcher.

"What's happening, Doc?" Katt asked.

"We've arrived at Leyte Gulf," Duffy said. "All the wounded are being transferred to a hospital ship. I don't want you walking. We'll come back and put you on a stretcher. Just be a couple of minutes."

Katt knew he'd never get back aboard the *Callahan* if they moved him to the hospital ship. He pushed himself up. He was a little dizzy at first, but it passed. He was barefoot and wearing someone else's T-shirt and dungaree trousers. There wasn't much time, and he needed a hiding place. Destroyers didn't have many of those. If he went aft, someone would see him. Out the forward wardroom door and to the right, he saw the open door to the XO's cabin. The XO was not there. Katt stepped in and looked around. The locker for the XO's clothes was six feet tall.

Katt opened the locker's double doors. It was wall to wall with uniforms on hangers. The floor was covered with shoes and small boxes.

Katt hurried back to the starboard forward corner of the wardroom where they'd laid him. His still-soggy clothes were in a pile against the starboard bulkhead. He left the T-shirt but took his dungaree trousers, blue shirt, and black socks. He dropped one sock amidships at the forward side of the wardroom table. The other sock he dropped next to the port side aft door. Then he took his trousers and shirt and returned to the XO's cabin. He pushed the XO's clothes aside and folded himself against the back wall of the locker. The handle on the front of the locker raised and lowered rods that slipped into slots to lock the doors. From inside the locker, Katt moved the locking rods into the locked position. Then he loaded his lap with shoes and boxes. Then he waited.

He heard a door open into the wardroom.

He heard, "He's gone, Doc." *Unger*, Katt thought. "You want me to look for him?"

"No goddamned time," Doc Duffy said. "The two amputees and the surviving burn victim need to get to the hospital ship ASAP."

Katt heard a door slam.

A minute later, "Petty Officer Katt, report to the fantail immediately," blared over the announcing system. The message was repeated. A minute later, Katt heard the grumble of a boat engine. Then he heard the anchor chain rattling in the hawse pipe. They were hauling up the anchor. Katt smiled.

Shortly, he felt the vibration of the propellers. The ship

was backing one propeller and going ahead on the other. "Twisting the ship," it was called. The officer of the deck twisted the ship to maneuver into or out of a tight space. The vibration stopped for a moment and then began again, but this time, it was indicative of moving forward.

Just a little longer, Katt thought. *Just keep the XO away for a little longer.*

The ship's announcing system blared, "Now set the underway refueling detail."

Katt hoped the XO didn't have something he needed for refueling. Then he wondered what would happen if the XO found him. He was a stowaway. And he was not at his appointed place of duty. He was supposed to be on the hospital ship.

He recalled the time he'd appeared at captain's mast back in 1941 in November. The CO had said, "You must be at your appointed place of duty, on goddamned time, every goddamned time!" He couldn't remember his first CO's last name. He couldn't recall if he'd ever known it. The man was the captain, Cap'n, or CO.

The CO who took over after Katt left, he remembered his name. He was Lieutenant Commander Drake. He wondered if he'd still be aboard. Maybe he too got a promotion and went to another job. Maybe Commander Drake wouldn't remember that Katt had pissed him off.

The ship had sped up. Now it was slowing. It probably meant they were sliding into position next to an oiler.

Katt opened the door and peered out. No one around. He climbed out, straightened the clothes and the shoes and boxes, and relocked the locker. The wardroom was empty. He exited through the aft door on the port side and descended a ladder to the First Division berthing space.

It too was deserted. He found a bunk with the mattress folded in half. Unassigned. The top one in a tier of three. He climbed up and lay on the folded mattress.

He'd been there a while when the ship's announcing system called, "Secure from refueling. Set the regular underway watch. On deck section one." A few minutes later, feet rattled down the ladder, and a familiar face passed Katt.

"Wyatt," Katt said.

"Jesus Christ. Scared the shit out of me, man." Wyatt glared at him. "Katt. People been looking for you. XO is getting ready to call a man-overboard muster."

"Lend me some clothes, please?"

Katt pulled on a pair of Wyatt's dungarees and folded cuffs into the legs. The shirtsleeves too had to be rolled up. And Wyatt's dress uniform shoes might not stay on his feet, but they'd have to do.

Katt hustled up to the pilothouse and told the boatswain mate of the watch who he was and asked if he could speak to the CO. The CO heard the exchange from his chair on the starboard side of the cramped space, and he motioned Katt to come forward.

"Captain," Katt said. "I stowed away, sort of."

The CO chuckled. "Sort of?"

Commander Drake looked different from that day back in Pearl when the *Callahan* was tying up to pier D1 after the *Yorktown* sank. Then he'd been a young, lean-faced man, the hair on the sides of his head under his hat coal black. Now his face was puffy. He had bags under his eyes, and his hair was gray on the sides, feathering gradually into black on top.

"If I went to the hospital ship, sir, I knew I'd never get back to the *Callahan*. I'd like to serve here, sir, if you'll have me."

"I remember you. That day in Pearl when you got to the Battle of Midway and I didn't."

Katt looked down at the deck, expecting the worst.

"Relax, Petty Officer Katt. If I'd had the guts to jump in the water and swim the way you did, I would have gone with you. Whatever the hell I was mad about back then doesn't mean anything anymore."

Katt met the CO's eyes. "You'll let me stay, sir?"

"In the history of the US Navy, I don't know if anyone ever shanghaied himself aboard a ship before. Welcome … welcome back aboard, shipmate." The captain turned in his chair. "Boatswain, see if you can find some clothes that fit this runt. He looks like a ragamuffin."

The *Callahan* steamed to Ulithi and tied up next to a repair ship. The ruined after gun mount was lifted off, and two pom-pom guntubs were welded into place. On December 12, with repairs completed, the *Callahan* departed Ulithi with two other destroyers as escorts for three oilers assigned to refuel part of Task Force Thirty-Eight, whose carrier planes were striking northern Luzon.

Katt had seen the number of US Navy ships involved in the Leyte Gulf operation. Hundreds. Hundreds more were anchored at Ulithi being repaired, altered, and replenished with ammo and supplies. Task Force Thirty-Eight, according to the word, consisted of three task groups. Each task group formed around three aircraft carriers. In 1942, an entire task force formed around one aircraft carrier. Then the rest of the force consisted of cruisers and destroyers. Now the battlewagons were back. The navy had been busy building new and restoring battle-damaged ships during '43 and '44, Katt mused. At the time, the *Callahan* was assigned to RG (replenishment group) 38.3. When RG 38.3 rendezvoused with Task Group 38.1, the *Callahan* would be assigned to TG 38.1. Some of the sailors expressed amazement that the US Navy had come up with such a clever way to keep track of all the ships committed to the Pacific war. Task forces, task groups. It made sense. The way sailors usually talked, it was "Situation Normal, All Fouled Up," and officers went to college to figure out how to shove their heads up their asses. The navy and *clever* in the same sentence: amazing!

On the second day of the four-day trip to the rendezvous, the day dawned with an overcast sky. Throughout the day, waves and swells increased. Katt was the 1600-to-2000 boatswain mate of the watch. He checked on the starboard lookout, Seaman First Wyatt, at 1900.

"You feel the way the ship is rolling?" Wyatt asked.

"Yeah. It's funny. On the *Dalton*, they said adding the radar made her top heavy, and it rolls different from before. 'Get used to it,' they said."

The ship did its funny jerky roll. Katt felt as if he were floating for a moment. Wyatt grabbed the bulwark.

"I'm not getting used to this," Wyatt said. "Before I came in the navy, my uncle bought me a ride in a barnstormer at the county fair. The pilot did something, and I felt like I was floating free, like I wasn't connected to the plane, like the plane wasn't connected to the air, like in a second I'd fall to the ground way down there and splatter like a egg."

Wyatt was right. It did feel as if the ship sometimes lost its grip on the water and had no way to right itself after a roll, but the lookout's job had nothing to do with worrying about how the ship rode in heavy weather.

"Japs won't be out here in weather like this," Katt said. "That's what they're thinking we're thinking. You got one job, Seaman Wyatt. Look out for Japs."

Whatever Wyatt mumbled was ripped away by the forty-five-knot winds.

When Katt reentered the pilothouse, he overheard the CO talking with the engineer. "Fuel state's 38 percent. We won't refuel till day after tomorrow. Hopefully this system blows over by then. Take on ballast."

The CO listened and then said, "I understand your concern about getting seawater contamination in the fuel if we ballast, but right now, we're steaming into a storm. If we have to turn and get the seas and wind on the beam, we're going to have a rough time. Flood the empty fuel tanks, and hop to it."

The next morning, during Katt's 0400-to-0800 watch, he thought the ship was riding better, though the winds had picked up to sixty knots.

Throughout the day and throughout the ship, things that were not welded into place clanged and rattled as the ship rolled and pitched. The ceaseless cacophony was as tiring as fighting for footing against the ship's motion. Eating was an adventure. The mess decks became greasy and slick with spilled food and drink, and a half-dozen casualties— sprained ankles, a cut lip, a concussion, and one broken arm—resulted from the hazardous dining conditions. Eventually, the cooks resorted to serving only cold cuts and bread. Most of the crew was happy to eat whatever was available; a few, however, tried not to think of food. Another few wanted to die to end the misery suffusing each and every cell of their bodies.

When Katt came back on watch at 1600, the winds had abated to less than forty knots. The waves and swells, however, continued to bob the flotilla of oilers and destroyers like toy boats in a rowdy boy's bathtub. Looking to the side, Katt watched another destroyer bury its bow in a wave as the sea covered five-inch gun mount number one. Then the bow shot up, tossing off the water, which the wind ripped away in a cloud of white spray. The lookouts took a beating, and Katt kept an eye on them.

At 1700, the replenishment group was ten miles from TG 38.1. The two groups were steaming directly at each other. RG 38.3 was going to have to reverse course.

"Boatswain," the officer of the deck said, "announce standby for heavy rolls."

Katt aye-ayed and picked up the microphone. He knew what the sailors would say as soon as he made the announcement. *You dumb shit, Katt, what the hell you think we been doing all damned day? Taking heavy rolls is what!* They'd bitch, but they'd hang on. Cooks would grab knives to keep them from flying around. Anyone handling ammo would make sure the explosives were secured.

During the turn, the *Callahan* snapped sudden vicious rolls one way and then reversed suddenly. Doc Duffy got two new patients: one with a broken collarbone and another with a crushed hand.

On the new southeasterly course, steaming with the seas, the ship exhibited new quirky behavior with rolling and pitching. The crew had become more cautious, however, and despite the CO worrying about fatigue from fighting prolonged violent ship motion affecting the crew, no other injuries occurred.

When Katt and Wyatt stomped up the ladder at 0340 for their morning watch, Wyatt bellyached about the unrelenting motion.

"When will this goddamned shit end, man? This has been going on like for months."

"Not even twenty-four hours," Katt pointed out.

"Feels like months."

Katt didn't think there was much point in getting angry at God or at His ocean. There was also no point to trying to talk Wyatt out of his funk. Not many sailors took things as Job had.

Not that I think I'm like him, Lord. That'd be prideful.

At 0410, the CO told Katt to announce that the ship would reverse course in five minutes, that all hands should brace for heavy rolls, and that sleeping sailors should be awakened.

Halfway through the turn, when the wind and seas aimed at the ship's beam, there was an anxious moment when the ship whipsawed back and forth and took a roll of forty-five degrees, and Katt experienced a second of that falling-into-space feeling before the ship shuddered back to upright. After the steadying on the northwesterly heading, the CO called the operations officer.

"Anything new from the fleet weatherman?" the CO asked. Katt couldn't hear the response. "We still have the same schedule, then—the carriers will launch strikes against Luzon airfields at sunup, and if we have no kamikaze threat, we refuel?" The CO listened for a moment, hung up, and dialed another number. "Chief Engineer, CO," he said. "Deballast." He hung up.

Sunrise was at 0615, but it didn't grow light enough to see the oiler fifteen hundred yards in front of them until 0730. At 0800, as the *Callahan* approached the oiler, Katt and two sailors huddled on the 01 level behind the superstructure housing the pilothouse. Knee-deep water washed over the main deck where they'd have to connect the refueling hose from the oiler. The three had safety lines tied to them. They wouldn't move down to the hazardous main deck until the last minute. First, the *Callahan* had to stabilize alongside the oiler. Then the oiler crew would fire a weighted line with a modified shotgun. With the line, the crew could haul a wire cable across the churning fifty feet of water separating the two vessels, and the refueling hose suspended from pulley wheels would ride on the cable over to the destroyer to receive life-sustaining fuel. Even in good weather, the operation was dangerous.

Katt had experienced refueling at sea a dozen times before—once in rough weather. Then it had seemed as if they'd never be able to accomplish the task in the wind and rain and water washing over the deck. But they had. They had gotten the job done, and no one had been hurt. Maybe it would work out that way this time too.

Please, God.

The stern of the oiler passed abeam Katt. The bow of the *Callahan* sank, and he felt a buzz through the hull. The screws had come out of the water and sped up. The oiler shot ahead. Then the stern of the *Callahan* sank, and the ship surged forward, passing the oiler's stern again. Suddenly, the destroyer veered toward the oiler. Katt thought a collision was certain, but the gray vessels separated as abruptly as they'd rushed toward each other.

Katt let out a held breath.

"Secure from refueling stations," blared over the ship announcing system. "On deck section three."

One of the sailors asked Katt, "We're not going to refuel?"

"Captain must have decided it was too dangerous," Katt replied.

Katt wasn't on watch, but he changed into dry clothes and climbed the ladder to the pilothouse. There wasn't room for extra people there, but something compelled him to go. The ship pitched, and he had to stop ascending as extra gravity pinned his feet to the steps. Then rolls threatened to toss him off the side of the ladder. The sea state had obviously gotten worse. But he adjusted to the up-and-down and sideways pushes and pulls and entered the pilothouse as a signalman reported through the voice tube, "Officer of the Deck, the flattop in front of us reports winds are seventy-five knots."

Katt couldn't see the carrier at first, but for an instant, the windshield wipers coped with rain and spray, and he saw the huge vessel maybe a mile in front. A blue plane ripped loose from the after part of the flight deck and tumbled into the sea tailfirst. Then the weather curtained off the view ahead. Out the starboard side, Katt could see two destroyers. They were submerged as much as afloat.

A radio speaker mounted to the overhead crackled

first, and then: "Task Group 38.1. Immediate execute. Turn starboard to new course one five zero."

The order was repeated, and the conning officer ordered the right turn.

"Stand by for heavy rolls announcement. Officer of the Deck?" the boatswain asked.

The OOD looked at the CO on his chair. The CO hesitated, and then he said, "Make it."

He sounded despondent, Katt thought.

Katt made the announcement.

Halfway through the turn, Katt looked out the port window and saw nothing but a wall of water. Katt grabbed onto the quartermaster's chart table as the wave hit and tilted the *Callahan* over sixty degrees. There was that moment of falling-off-the-earth sensation again. The ship staggered back to near upright. Another wave hit and shoved her over hard again. Again the ship struggled back to nearly upright.

A third wave hit. Katt lost his grip on the table. He wound up sitting on his butt on the ceiling, the overhead.

A couple of guys moaned. He saw the CO jumbled into a pile underneath his chair. His neck was bent funny.

Katt pushed himself to his knees and crossed himself. *Don't let the Japs kill me. My prayer. You answered it.* He was awed by the realization.

He looked up at the deck above him. There was like a hole of light in the dark, and he saw Sister Ralph in third grade. She was talking about souls. She smiled, and he smiled back.

The bridge windows shattered. The sea cascaded in.

13

OCTOBER 1946

It was the Tuesday before Halloween. Mrs. Grossman sat at the desk in the walled-off post office corner of her store. She looked at the letter in her hand. It had been months, three, she thought, since the last government letter had come for Wanda Katt. She tapped the letter on the palm of her hand.

"Otto," she called through the barred window. "Ach, that boy," she muttered and thought of Preston and how she'd never had a boy work like he did. "Otto!" she yelled louder.

Something crashed in the storeroom. The boy had probably been sleeping.

The tousled blond head appeared at the barred window.

"Take this to Miss Katt," Mrs. Grossman said. "Then come back here. Directly back here, *verstehe?*"

"Sure," Otto said. "I understand."

Otto skipped out and ran past the storefront window.

Mrs. Grossman spun her chair and glanced at the bulletin board, which held Preston's medals and a piece of paper listing all the battles and campaigns he'd fought in.

Such a shame, she thought as she always did when reminded of him. *He goes through a dozen battles and his ship sinks in a storm. Such a shame. Only 13 men of 231 survived. Preston was not one of them. Such a shame.*

She rose and went to the bulletin board and touched the GUADALCANAL line on the paper. Then she put a light fingertip on each of his medals.

As soon as he cleared the storefront window, Otto stopped running. He did not want to go to the Katt woman's house again. When he delivered the death notice in January of '45, she'd screamed at him. "Where's the government life insurance? He had a policy. He wrote me. Where is it? Did you steal it, you evil little snot?"

Otto ran.

Two months ago, another envelope and a small package came for Mrs. Katt. Again, he did not want to go back to that creepy house across the creek, but Mrs. Grossman insisted. He knocked on the door, shivering, though it was hot and humid. After Mrs. Katt tore the package open and found nothing but medals in it, she jammed the contents back in the box and threw them at Otto.

She pointed a dirty, long-nailed finger at him. "You'd better bring me my government life insurance check the next time you come." She looked like a witch. "Pick that up and git."

And Otto did.

By the time he reached the bridge over Verrückt Frau Creek, he'd decided. He was not going back to that house. Looking at it from the middle of the bridge, it was scary enough. The woman never came into the store. Mrs. Grossman would never find out. He closed his eyes, imagining opening his hand and watching the envelope flutter like a leaf to the water to be carried down the creek to the Mississippi River and from there all the way to the Gulf of Mexico. He opened his eyes. He still held the envelope. Turning around, he saw the top of the church steeple above Grossman's Farm Implements store. If he dropped the envelope, he'd have to confess it.

Facing the house again, Otto wondered why a boy had to do penance even for sins he didn't commit. With his heart rate kicking up, he crossed the bridge and began saying Our Fathers and Hail Marys. Most of the time, his penance was five of each. He was on his fourth Hail Mary when he stopped halfway through the prayer. It was quiet at the rear of the house, as if even the birds and bugs stopped what they were doing to see what would happen next. He rapped on the door. The sound scared him even though he made it.

The hinges creaked as the door jerked open. Miss Katt's evil black eyes nailed Otto to the packed dirt. His legs couldn't obey his urgent wish to run.

Mrs. Katt's gray skin stretched tightly over her sunken cheeks. Otto tried to swallow, but he couldn't.

"What?" the raspy voice demanded.

Otto held up the envelope.

She snatched it from him and checked the return address, and her lips curled up in a smile of the kind a jack-o'-lantern would wear. She ripped open the envelope and pulled out a check. Her face seemed to light up for an instant. Then the woman's face grew scary again.

"What is it?" a man's voice from inside asked.

"You waiting for a tip?" she snarled.

Otto shook his head, his eyes locked onto the woman's.

"What the hell you got there?" the man asked from behind her and spun her around.

"Nothing!" she screeched. "A bill."

The man slapped her, and Otto ran around the house, along the levee, and across the bridge.

The one-story Saint Ambrose Bank snuggled between two-story Grossman's Farm Implements and two-story Ollie's Tavern. Just before lunchtime, Wanda Katt entered and presented a check for $5,000 to the teller.

"You want to open a savings account, Mrs. Katt?" the teller asked.

"Give her the money," the man with her said.

The cashier didn't know the man. He had black hair gone to gray on the sides and wore faded work clothes. His chin sported little bits of toilet paper where he'd nicked himself shaving. *A hobo from the train, probably,* the cashier thought. The railroad delivered grain cars to the elevator at the east end of town. Otherwise, the trains never even slowed down passing through Saint Ambrose. Since the thirties, bums had been getting off the freight trains at the elevator. Since the thirties, townspeople had been locking their doors at night.

"This much money, you ought to open a savings account," the cashier said again. "It'll earn interest."

"Give it."

The man seemed to grow taller and scarier. The teller looked at Mrs. Katt, questions written all over his face.

"We're getting married," Wanda Katt said.

"I have to see Mr. Wetzal," the cashier said.

"Then see him," the man growled.

Mr. Wetzal came out to the counter from an office in the rear. He suggested a savings account also, but the betrothed couple insisted on cash.

When the five stuffed envelopes were placed on the counter, the man snatched them up. He extracted a bill from one and handed it to Wanda. "Groceries," he said. The man himself walked next door to Ollie's and bought a case of gin.

About one the next morning, Mrs. Ohlenschlager, with a coal-oil lantern in hand, was halfway from her Second Street house to her outhouse when she noticed the glow from the west. She wondered if she'd read the clock wrong but then realized the sun rose in the east. *A fire!*

She woke her husband. He woke others, but there was nothing they could do. The Katt house had burned to the stone foundation. It took a day for the place to cool down enough to discover the two bodies, one female, the other male. Wanda Katt and Toilet-Paper Chin, they figured.

Two years later, the Saint Ambrose Volunteer Fire Brigade was formed. Emil Grossman was the first fire chief.

Mrs. Grossman maintained her "Preston Katt Bulletin Board" in the post office until 1955. That's when the Grossmans built a new grocery store with a separate building for a post office. A two-story American Legion Post was built across Main Street from the Grossmans' new store to honor Korean War veterans. Mr. Grossman insisted on that. The hall on the second floor with the huge dance floor was named Preston Katt Hall. Mrs. Grossman insisted on that.

ABOUT THE AUTHOR

J. J. Zerr is a United States Navy veteran who holds a master's degree in Engineering. J. J. resides in Missouri. He previously published three other books, *The Ensign Locker*, *Sundown Town Duty Station*, and *Noble Deeds*.

CPSIA information can be obtained at www.ICGtesting.com
Printed in the USA
LVOW08s1315050515

437186LV00001B/1/P